OLIVIA
THE RUNAWAY
VICTORIAN ROMANCE

Catharine Dobbs

Copyright © 2021 by Catharine Dobbs.

All rights reserved. No part of this publication may be reproduced, distributed or transmitted in any form or by any means, including photocopying, recording, or other electronic or mechanical methods, without the prior written permission of the publisher, except in the case of brief quotations embodied in critical reviews and certain other noncommercial uses permitted by copyright law.

Publisher's Note: This is a work of fiction. Names, characters, places and incidents are a product of the author's imagination. Locales and public names are sometimes used for atmospheric purposes. Any resemblance to actual people, living or dead, or to businesses, companies, events, institutions, or locales is completely coincidental.

Contents

Prologue That Fateful Night..5

Chapter 1 Craddock's Correction House................................8

Chapter 2 A Useful Mouse..16

Chapter 3 A Bit of Luck 22

Chapter 4 Where is the Gold? 33

Chapter 5 Mr. Artemis Gobler 44

Chapter 6 The Art of the Pickpocket....................................59

Chapter 7 An Uncomfortable Plan.......................................67

Chapter 8 A Clatter in the Night!...76

Chapter 9 An Unexpected Turn 86

Chapter 10 A Past Reminder..97

Chapter 11 A Family to Call Her Own 105

Chapter 12 A Delightful Surprise 117

Chapter 13 Miss Elizabeth Tupple 126

Chapter 14 At Home with Arthur 133

Chapter 15 An Extraordinary Revelation 151

Chapter 16 Surprises in Kent 160

Chapter 17 The Guest of Honour.......................................171

Prologue
That Fateful Night

The baby's screams filled the house, echoing through the corridors, as a storm raged outside. The nursemaid was doing her best to quieten the child, knowing the rage into which her master would fly if he were to hear it. She hushed it, as her mistress lay upon the bed, exhausted from the birth, her brow sweating, the blood-stained sheets lying all around.

"The child is healthy, ma'am," the nursemaid whispered, cradling the baby in her arms.

"A boy?" the woman asked, and the nursemaid shook her head.

"No, ma'am, a girl, a healthy girl. Will you hold her?" the nursemaid asked, bringing the baby to her mistresses' arms.

"What a beautiful little thing you are," she said, taking the baby to her breast as she struggled to sit up.

"Take care not to exhaust yourself, ma'am, you are still weak from the birth. Do you see the birthmark there?" the nursemaid said, "she is special, I can tell."

The child had a small mark on her upper arm, almost in the shape of a cross, as though she were blessed.

"She is perfect," the woman replied.

"That she is, ma'am, as perfect as her mother. She will be the gentlest of creatures, I am sure," the nursemaid said.

"I feel … I feel unwell," the woman said, and she fell back upon the bed, as the nursemaid took the baby from her.

"You must rest, ma'am. I will take care of … what will you call her?" she asked, and the woman gave a weak smile.

"Olivia, she is to be called Olivia," she said, before closing her eyes and sighing with deep exhaustion.

***

But Olivia's fate lay far from the happy world into which her own mother had grown up, destined to a life which bore little resemblance to that in which she had been born; an unfortunate birth, one which she paid for dearly. Lady Beatrice Tupple, her mother, was the youngest daughter of Lord and Lady Artemis Tupple of Kent, great landowners, and philanthropists, his Lordship being heir to a considerable estate with fortune and title.

She had fallen in love with the undergardener on her father's estate, a handsome man by the name of Joseph Bayly, a man who had enchanted her, and for whom she held nothing but love. When the affair was discovered, they sent him away in disgrace, an act which broke Beatrice's heart and left her a mere shadow of her former self.

But Joseph left something more than memories, and when it was discovered that Beatrice was with child, her father flew into an even greater rage. He confined her to the house, employing a nursemaid to watch over her until the child's arrival was due. Beatrice longed for Joseph, but her father and mother, horrified by the scandal which would ensue if the child were discovered, decreed that when it was born it should be taken away.

There had been only one other witness to the birth that night, Beatrice's younger sister Elizabeth. She was only fourteen years old, watching quietly at the door as her sister cradled the newborn baby in her arms. Lord and Lady Tupple had wished nothing to do with it, making no enquiry as to their daughter's health, save to ask if the baby was yet delivered so that it might be taken away.

On that stormy night, as rain lashed against the windows of the grand house and the wind howled all around, they secreted a bundle out into the darkness. Olivia was to be raised far away, the affair pushed aside and forgotten, the scandal avoided. Elizabeth had caught only a glimpse of the baby, and Beatrice had barely had a moment to say goodbye. She had wept as they carried away the child; the screams of the baby once more echoing through the house.

"What will become of her?" Elizabeth had asked, and the nursemaid had shaken her head sadly.

"Only our prayers can go with her, miss," she had replied, as Beatrice had struggled to the window of the attic room in which she had given birth.

From there, through the darkness, she had made out the shadow of a horseman riding off into the night, the bundle of the baby in a basket at his front.

"Goodbye, my sweet little darling," she had whispered, as tears rolled down her cheeks.

Olivia was gone, and her life to come would surely differ greatly from the life she had but for a few moments enjoyed.

Chapter 1
Craddock's Correction House

Olivia had pricked her finger a dozen times that afternoon. She was sitting at a long table, mending smocks, watched over by the all-seeing eye of Mrs. Dounce, who had chastised her that day as often as she had pricked her finger.

"Silly little girl, have I not shown you often enough how to thread properly? I think you do it deliberately," she said, cuffing Olivia around the ear and snatching her sewing from her.

"Please, Mrs. Dounce, I am tired," Olivia replied, to which Mrs. Dounce responded by cuffing her again.

"And do you not think that I might be tired too, Olivia? You are nothing but a wicked and ungrateful child. We feed you, clothe you, give you a bed and the warm comforts of a home, and all we ask in return is for you to work your way. It pains me to see such disobedient children," she said, shaking her head, as she threw down the sewing and cuffed Olivia once again.

The comfortable home which Mrs. Dounce spoke of was neither homely nor comfortable, at least not for those children unfortunate enough to find themselves resident there. Olivia was seven years old, and she had lived at Craddock's Correction House for as long as she could remember. It was a grim and foreboding place, once a great stately house, now fallen into disrepair.

Around a hundred orphans lived there, watched over by Mr. and Mrs. Dombus Dounce, a couple for whom comfort was paramount, hence their belief that Craddock's Correction House was comfortable for all. They lived in considerable luxury, their size and demeanour suggesting as much, their table always well laden whilst the orphans survived on a diet of gruel and biscuits.

Olivia knew little about her past, only that her future appeared as bleak as the present in which she lived. She slept in the dormitory with fifty other girls, their beds pushed close together, mice and rats, their night-time companions. Every day, except on a Sunday, they forced the children to work in the appalling conditions of the sewing shop or the mill where machines whirred and clickety-clacked, and fingers easily lost to injury.

It was a harsh and unforgiving life, but Olivia knew no different. She was used to the cruelty of Mrs. Dounce, the angry outbursts from Mr. Dounce, and the relentless drudge of daily life which ground the orphans down like wheat in the mill. Now, she sighed, picking up her sewing and rethreading the needle. She had a pile of smocks to finish, and another pile of breeches to hem, her hands red-raw and sore from her efforts.

"Again! I will not have it," a shout came from the doorway of the sewing workshop and Mr. Dounce appeared, dragging another little girl by the scruff of her neck.

Olivia looked up in alarm as Mrs. Dounce rushed forward to take hold of the child who was struggling in her husband's grip.

"Let me go," she shouted, and Mrs. Dounce cuffed her around the ear, a favourite practice of hers to deal with just about any misdemeanour the orphans could present.

"And what has Mabel Marie done now, Mr. Dounce?" his wife asked, as the orphanage governor shook his head solemnly.

He was almost as wide as he was tall, with a red face and five separate chins, an ill-fitting wig perched precariously upon his head. His wife looked little different, and together they presented what would have been a most comical appearance had it not been for the unpleasant punishments they were more than capable of enacting.

"What do you think, Mrs. Dounce? She tries to escape. Again," he said, shaking his head, as Mabel Marie struggled in his arms.

She was Olivia's best friend, a small child, gaunt, with wide blue eyes and long brown hair, a contrast to Olivia's blonde curls and deep green eyes, the two of them inseparable. But Mabel Marie harboured a desire which often got her into trouble, the desire to escape the orphanage and go in search of her mother, whom she knew had abandoned her when she was five years old.

"You naughty little girl," Mrs. Dounce said, grabbing Olivia from her husband and hurrying along the work benches to where Olivia was still trying to thread her needle.

"Please, Mrs. Dounce, I just want to find my mama," Mabel Marie said, for which she received a fresh cuff around the ear.

"Your mama is gone, she does not want you, that is why we are to have the unfortunate task of caring for you. You are nothing but an ungrateful little wench," Mrs. Dounce said, as the rows of orphans fell silent, staring round at Mabel Marie, who now cried.

Olivia put her arm around her, as her sobs echoed around the workshop.

"Back to work," Mr. Dounce shouted, bringing his fist down hard upon the workbench.

Around them, the other orphans resumed their duties, the sounds of the weaving looms clacketing in the air once again.

"What happened?" Olivia asked, as Mabel Marie wiped her eyes.

"I nearly did it this time, but he caught me by the water pump. If I had only been a moment sooner, then I would have been through the hedge and away," she said, shaking her head.

"But you cannot keep doing this, the punishment will be worse every time. You know that," Olivia said, and Mabel Marie shook her head.

"I do not care, Olivia, I want to find my mama. She is in London, I know she is," Mabel Marie replied.

"Get on with your work, Olivia," Mrs. Dounce shouted, and the two girls resumed their tasks.

London had always held an attraction for Mabel Marie. It was there that she believed her mother to have gone after she left her at the orphanage, a place which some said had streets lined with gold. The myth of London hung heavily in the air of Craddock's Correction House, the older orphans often speaking of making their fortune there, though no one really knew the truth of what it was like to go there.

London lay some fifty miles from the orphanage, and Olivia had travelled barely further than the outskirts of the non-descript little town in which she lived. She spent her days at work, on Sundays she went to church, and once a year an outing was arranged into the countryside, where the children would picnic and play games at the expense of a charitable guild which sought to ease the grinding poverty of the lower classes.

Her life was ordered and determined, far from any hopes she might ordinarily have had in other circumstances. Occasionally she would wonder about herself, who she was and where she had come from. Mabel Marie had memories of her mother, but Olivia had nothing of the sort, destined, it seemed, to know nothing of her past. She would invent stories about herself, imagining that she was descended from royalty or that her parents were away on some marvellous adventure. But such fantasies were only dreams, and when she had dared to ask Mrs. Dounce who her mother was, she had met her with a flat refusal.

"You do not need to know such things. We know nothing of you, Olivia. You were brought here as a baby and here you shall remain under our charity. It is a sad fact that so many parents bring children into the world and then find themselves unable to take care of them. Thank goodness for those, like Mr. Dounce and I, willing to sacrifice so much for the greater good," she had said, and that had been the end of the conversation.

But Olivia had always wondered about her mother and father. Who were they? And what had made them abandon her to a place like Craddock's Correction House?

"Promise me you will not try to escape again, Mabel Marie," Olivia whispered, as the two girls sat sewing at their workbenches.

"But I have to. I cannot stay here, not any longer," Mabel Marie replied.

"Then do not do it without me," Olivia replied, for Mabel Marie was her only friend in all the world, and the thought of losing her was just too dreadful to bear.

"Would you really come with me?" Mabel Marie replied, and Olivia nodded.

"You know I would. I hate this place as much as you do, as much as we all do," she said, and Mabel Marie smiled.

"All right then, I promise," she said, just as Mrs. Dounce brought her hand down hard on the desk in front of them.

"Enough! Disobedient little girls get no supper. I shall have you sent to bed hungry. It is no more than you deserve, the both of you," she said, and wobbled off along the row of benches, cuffing the other orphans as she went, believing her hold over them all to be complete.

***

Olivia and Mabel Marie barely noticed the absence of supper. It was a menial meal of thin gruel and bread. On Sundays there would be scraps of bacon to go with it, but on any other night the meagre rations provided little sustenance. They sent the two girls up to the dormitory where they lay upon their beds side by side and talked of their dreams and hopes for the future.

"Perhaps we could slip out at night," Olivia said, and Mabel Marie shook her head.

"The doors are all locked and Mrs. Dounce stalks the corridors in the early hours. You know she has trouble sleeping. Do you remember when she caught Charlie in the larder?" Mabel Marie said, and Olivia nodded.

Charlie Nichols had slipped unseen into the kitchens, retrieving a large fruit cake from the Dounce's own larder, only to be discovered returning to the dormitories. He had stood out in the orphanage yard, for it was winter then, barefooted and with nothing but his pyjamas to protect him from the cold. Mr. Dounce had made an example of him, one which the other orphans were unlikely to forget, the poor boy having caught a chill which lasted the entire season long.

"She would know we were trying to escape," Olivia said, and Mabel Marie nodded.

"We could slip away during the day. I nearly got away with it today, I really did. Mr. Dounce usually takes a knap after lunch, but today he was shouting at the farm lad who brings the eggs, something about half of them being cracked. He had waited for him, that is why I got caught," Mabel Marie said.

"But now, Mrs. Dounce will be carefully observing you. If she sees that the two of us are gone, then she will know immediately what has happened," Olivia said, and both girls sighed.

"I just want to get to London, I want to see the golden pavements and find my mother," Mabel Marie said.

"But do you really think she will be there? What if it is not like that at all?" Olivia said, for she found it hard to believe that London was anything like Mabel Marie described it, as much as she might wish it to be.

"In London, everything will be well, I just know it will be," Mabel Marie said, and Olivia did not like to disabuse her friend, for she too had dreams of a better life, far away from the orphanage and the cruelty of Mr. and Mrs. Dounce.

Olivia had once watched from the orphanage window as a cart carrying a farming family had passed by. The man had been tall and handsome, his wife round and rosy with a beautiful smile upon her face. Two children had ridden with them, a girl and a boy, each with smiles upon their faces, laughing and joking with one another. It was a picture which had long stayed with Olivia, one which she had dreamed of being hers.

The thought of escaping Craddock's Correction House had long been in her mind, but where would she go? What would she do? London seemed such a long way away, a place which, far from being paved with gold, could easily be the place of her downfall. But there was a determination in Mabel Marie, a longing for something more than the dull drudgery of the orphanage, a longing which Olivia too possessed.

"Then we must think long and hard," Olivia said, as the sounds of the other orphans returning to the dormitories echoed up the stairs.

"Do you promise?" Mabel Marie asked, and Olivia nodded.

"With all my heart," she said, and the two girls embraced, knowing that their future lay together, an adventure just beginning.

Chapter 2
A Useful Mouse

Olivia had just finished hemming a pile of breeches, and Mrs. Dounce picked one up to inspect it, holding the line up to the light and tutting.

"These are not good enough, Olivia. Do them again," she said, tossing the pair down on the workbench.

"But I did them as straight as I could," Olivia said, and Mrs. Dounce brought her hand down hard in front of her.

"How dare you question me? They are wrong, Olivia, wrong, wrong, wrong, and if I say they are wrong, then they are wrong. Do you understand?" Mrs. Dounce said, and Olivia nodded.

"Yes, Mrs. Dounce," she said, and with a sigh she unpicked the pair she had just finished sewing.

They sat Mabel Marie opposite her, threading a needle, and the two exchanged glances, as Mrs. Dounce started shouting at another of the orphans behind them.

"She is getting worse by the day," Mabel Marie whispered.

"I hate her," Olivia replied, as she caught her finger on the needle she had just threaded, the blood running onto the breeches she was about to hem.

"Foolish girl, get up," Mrs. Dounce cried, dragging Olivia to her feet, "look at what you have done. You have ruined them, think of what you have cost us, you ungrateful girl."

"Please, Mrs. Dounce, I did not mean to," Olivia said, but Mrs. Dounce had already dragged her from the workbench and through the workshop, chastising her they went.

"I have never known such ungratefulness," Mrs. Dounce said, as they left the workshop, and they hurried Olivia along the corridor toward Mr. Dounce's office.

His wife hammered upon the door and there was the sound of a ledger being closed before Mr. Dounce himself appeared before them. He looked annoyed at being disturbed, looking Olivia up and down with disdain, as his wife gabbled the reason for the interruption.

"I have had enough of this child. She has ruined a pair of breeches; she cannot sew and does not try to learn. Why do we put up with her, Mr. Dounce? Why?" his wife said, and Mr. Dounce looked at Olivia with a ponderous expression, chewing his top lip and sucking in a deep breath.

"These children are all the same, Mrs. Dounce, ungrateful. We shall see how she likes a day at the ledger, perhaps then she will reconsider her fondness for the sewing needle. Inside," he said, and grabbing Olivia by the ear, he pulled her into his office.

It was a large room lined with bookshelves, and at its centre there lay a substantial desk, covered in papers and documents. The window faced out onto Mr. and Mrs. Dounce's private garden, where the first spring roses were blooming, and lavender grew amidst box hedge and small, ornate trees.

"See that we put her to work, Mr. Dounce. Teach her some manners and discipline," Mrs. Dounce said, and slammed the door behind her.

"Well now, what shall we do with you," he said, as Olivia stood meekly in the centre of the room.

"Please Mr. Dounce, I …" Olivia began, but he raised his hand.

"It was not a question which required an answer. Now, sit down over here," he said, pointing to a small desk in the corner.

He rummaged around in a draw and brought out blank paper and ink, setting them down in front of her.

"But … I do not know how to write," she said, and he laughed.

"No, of course you do not. Which is why this day will be all the more humiliating for you. You will copy from this book, and if you make a mistake, you will begin again. In that way perhaps you learn mistakes should be avoided rather than atoned for," he said, placing an enormous book in front of her and opening it at the first page.

Olivia looked down at the unidentifiable marks on the page. She knew they were words, but her mind could not replace the marks with words, the letters appearing alien to her. With a shaking hand she took up the quill, dipping it into the ink, just as she had seen others do. If Olivia could not read, then she could certainly not write. The lessons imparted to the orphans by the curate, Mr. Lucas Houlding, extended only so far as the simplest of Bible stories.

"I do not know how to write," she whispered, and Mr. Dounce brought his face down close to hers.

"Then learn," he snarled, pointing to the blank page.

Olivia raised the quill, a drop of ink splattering upon the page. She tried to copy the first letter on the page, the quill feeling awkward. It should be easy, she told herself, but with Mr. Dounce watching over her, and having never been taught her letters, the task seemed impossible.

"I ... I do not know how," she whispered, and he brought his hand down hard upon the desk, causing her to jump.

"Then would it not be better to do those things you knew how? You know how to sew, do you not? Then practice. You know how to darn, do you not? Then practice. You know how to work the looms and the other machines, do you not? Then practice. Idle, that is what you, are, that is what all you orphans are," he said, snatching the quill from Olivia's hand.

"Please, Mr. Dounce. I did not mean to ..." she began, but he cuffed her about the ear and dragged her to her feet.

"You do not know how to read or to write. You are good only for what we have deemed fit for you to be good at. Now, go back to it and tell Mrs. Dounce that your cure has been effective. If I hear you have caused trouble again this day, then it will be the belt for you, my girl. Do you understand?" he said, pulling open his office door.

Olivia did not need to respond, pushed, as she was, through the door where she tripped and fell into the corridor. The door slammed behind her and she picked herself up, as tears welled up in her eyes. She felt humiliated, just as Mr. Dounce had intended. Slowly, she returned to the sewing workshop, where Mrs. Dounce sat her away from Mabel Marie and threatened her with a beating should she put a single foot out of line for the rest of the day.

"Are you all right?" Mabel Marie whispered to her, as she passed her by later that afternoon.

"We have to escape, we have to," Olivia replied, and Mabel Marie could only agree.

***

Later that evening, when supper had concluded, the children were in their dormitories. Mr. and Mrs. Dounce gave little thought to them enjoying their own lavish entertainments in their private quarters, the children left to fend for themselves until morning, unless trouble should occur.

The boy's dormitory was next to the girl's, joined by a door which was supposed to be locked but was always open. In this way, there was much back and forth, silly games and pranks played, the children making their own entertainment as best they could. Olivia and Mabel Marie sat upon Olivia's bed, talking, as they always did, of London and their plans to escape.

"It was just so horrible. The way he made me write, even though I cannot," Olivia said, still reeling from her ordeal at the hands of Mr. Dounce.

"They are both as cruel as one another. I hate them," Olivia said, as a cry of delight came from the far end of the dormitory, and several of the children hurried to see what the excitement was all about.

"It is Charlie and his tame mice," one girl said, and Olivia and Mabel Marie followed the crowd to watch Charlie, the hero of the fruit cake, display his pet mice.

He had tamed four of them, which he kept in a cage beneath his bed, and now they were balancing along a pole, each following the other before jumping into Charlie's outstretched hands.

"And see, this one even does a somersault," Charlie said, holding up one of his mice, which now jumped down from his hands and rolled across the floor.

He was a tall boy, a few years older than Olivia and Mabel Marie, with ginger hair, wide hazel eyes, and freckles across his nose.

"Make them walk again, Charlie," one boy said, but Charlie shook his head.

"I will tomorrow. They need their rest now. You cannot push performers like this, you know," he said, scooping up the mice, as a groan went up from the crowd of children, who now dispersed back to their beds.

"Are they really tame?" Mabel Marie asked, and Charlie nodded.

"Of course, they are. They always come back to me, wherever they have been," he said, and Olivia watched with fascination, as the mice sat happily upon Charlie's shoulder.

"I wish I had one," Mabel Marie said, turning to Olivia, who now took a deep breath.

"Can we borrow one?" she said, and Charlie looked at her in surprise.

"Borrow one? But whatever for?" he asked, and Olivia whispered in Mabel Marie's ear.

"Of course," she cried, "what a wonderful thought, Olivia. Yes, may we borrow one?" and Charlie scratched his head.

"I suppose so, but whatever for?" he said, and checking that no one else was listening, Olivia explained her plan.

Chapter 3
A Bit of Luck

For six days of every week, the children of Craddock's Correctional House worked, and on the sabbath they rested. At least, that is what Mr. and Mrs. Dounce would claim. 'Rest' was not a word the children knew, or if they did, it meant something quite different to the 'work' of the sabbath which they were forced to endure. In the morning, they would go to church, where an interminably long sermon by the curate would be followed by the litany and a lunch of mildly more substantial gruel than was offered on the weekdays. Following this, the orphanage would be cleaned, a task as back breaking as any of the 'work' the children undertook during the week. Thus, the sabbath was a day, not of rest, but of different endurance, enough to break up the week before regular duties resumed.

It was the Sunday after Olivia's ordeal at the hands of Mr. Dounce, and she and Mabel Marie were waiting patiently for the call to church. The children would walk in file, hand in hand, before being seated at the back of Saint Hildegard's, Mrs. Dounce making any number of threats toward them should they dare to set a foot out of line. She herself would take her usual pew and it would not be long before the sound of her snoring could be heard by all the orphans, much to their amusement. The source of her fatigue came from the sermon of the curate who liked to preach interminably on the finer points of scriptural exegesis.

"Have you got it?" Olivia whispered, and Mabel Marie nodded.

"Charlie handed it to me after breakfast. It's here in my pocket," she replied, and slipping her hand into her pocket she brought out one of Charlie's mice, which sniffed at the air and gazed around in surprise.

"Come along now, children, we do not wish to be later," Mrs. Dounce called out, and Mabel Marie hastily replaced the mouse in her pocket, as she and Olivia joined hands and followed the other orphans out into the sunshine.

It was a bright spring day, a gentle breeze bringing the scent of flowers upon the air, and the children walked happily together toward the church. Much of the town had gathered, the church bells ringing and Mr. Houlding waiting to welcome them, dressed in a billowing white surplice and preaching scarf.

"Ah, the Craddock's children," he said, beaming down at them, "welcome, welcome."

They filed into the church, where the smell of dust and flowers came over them, the organ playing a low tune, as Mrs. Dounce directed them to their usual pews.

"Be quiet now, you are in the church, show some respect," she said, settling herself down in the front pew, as the orphans sat quietly waiting for the service to begin.

The first hymn was *All Things Bright and Beautiful,* which was sung with much gusto by the congregation, the organ booming out across the church as the curate processed toward the front, his surplice billowing behind him. Olivia glanced at Mabel Marie. The two of them sat together on the end of a pew right at the back.

"During the sermon," Olivia whispered, and Mabel Marie smiled.

"And then the gold-paved streets," she said, as a haughty looking woman nearby glared at them both.

As the organ subsided, Mr. Houlding cleared his throat, opening his prayer book and read the sentences, as Mrs. Dounce stifled a yawn.

"When the wicked man turneth away from his wickedness that he hath committed, and doeth that which is lawful and right, he shall save his soul alive," he said, in the voice he reserved for church services, high pitched and monotonous.

Olivia smiled to herself, knowing that Mrs. Dounce would soon be asleep, only to be awakened in the rudest of manners.

"Wait until she is asleep," Olivia whispered, and Mabel Marie nodded.

They had listened to the scripture readings and Mr. Houlding had just climbed up into the pulpit, adjusting his spectacles and shuffling his notes.

"Ah, now where was I … ah yes, Ezekiel chapter seven, verse eight. A text of wrath, God is angry, we read in the commentaries, and here I shall quote the Greek directly …" he began, as members of the congregation visibly disengaged themselves, Mrs. Dounce amongst them.

It was the same every Sunday, and they would be lucky if Mr. Houlding's sermon lasted less than half an hour. His tone was interminably dull, helped little by his subject matter, the curate having the ability to select the most tedious portions of scripture, and say a great deal without saying anything at all.

Olivia watched as Mrs. Dounce's head nodded forward. It came around ten minutes into the sermon, just as Mr. Houlding was explaining the fine detail between the Greek translation of 'wrath' and 'anger,' which, according to his assessment, were very different things and should be considered as such.

"Now," Olivia said, and Mabel Marie slipped her hand into her pocket.

The plan was a simple one, though not without its risks, and she took out the mouse they had borrowed from Charlie, slipping it down to the floor where it scuttled along the aisle and made directly for a group of excitable young ladies from the local finishing school.

The scream which erupted from the nearest of them caused Mr. Houlding to look up in surprise. He was not used to such interruptions, and peered over his spectacles in astonishment, as the section of the congregation containing the girls from Miss Faverfew's school erupted into squeals.

There was much leaping and shrieking, as the mouse made its way amongst them, with several of the ladies clambering onto the pews. The disturbance caused a general panic about the church, as ladies in long skirts hitched them up and gentlemen took to their feet, lest the creature should scuttle up their trouser legs.

"Verger, quickly open the doors, it is only a mouse," Mr. Houlding called out, for he was no doubt eager to return to the subject in hand, his notes being barely on the third page.

The orphans had all taken great delight in the spectacle, rising to their feet, and craning their necks, as the young ladies danced about and screamed. Mrs. Dounce tried to quieten them, first with admonishment for disturbing the peace of God's house and secondly with threats of a most unchristian nature.

But her chastisements were to no avail, and the church was soon in uproar, as the mouse made its way from pew to pew, disappearing and reappearing in an alarmingly unpredictable fashion. They had thrown the doors open, and the verger was now in a state of anxious frenzy, chasing the mouse along the aisle, as the curate called for calm.

"Now, Olivia," Mabel Marie said, and the two girls slipped out of the church, hurrying through the graveyard and out onto the lane.

They did not stop until they had come to the little bridge which crossed the brook, close to the inn called *The Duke's Arms*. Here, they paused, catching their breath, and grinning at one another.

"We have done it, Olivia, we got away," Mabel Marie said, as Olivia glanced back toward the church.

There was no sign of anyone following them, and all was quiet along the lane, the grim façade of the orphanage lying off to their left across the meadows and the lane toward London beckoning them forward.

"So, what now?" Olivia asked, for the two of them had been so caught up in their plans to escape that the thought of what came next had hardly occurred.

"Well, we go to London, of course," Mabel Marie said, as though doing so would be the easiest thing in the world.

"They will surely come looking for us," Olivia said, and Mabel Marie took her by the arm.

"Then we must hurry and keep well hidden. Come on, our adventure has begun," she said, and the two of them ran off along the lane, Olivia casting a final glance back at the orphanage and wondering what her life was now to be.

***

They had brought nothing for the journey, since doing so would surely have aroused Mrs. Dounce's suspicions. They had with them only the clothes they stood up in and a small piece of bread which each had secreted at supper the night before. It was fortunate that it was early spring, the sun warm upon their backs and not a cloud in the sky above.

They made their way along the lane, soon leaving the town behind and making for the road which Mabel Marie had suggested would lead to London. Neither of them knew where they were going, but it felt good to be free at last, though secretly each worried how soon they might be discovered and taken back.

Olivia knew that if Mr. and Mrs. Dounce were to find them, then the punishment would be severe. Still, it had been a risk she was willing to take, confident that it would be some time before their disappearance was discovered. For the rest of the day, they hurried on through the lanes and byways, pausing by babbling brooks for refreshment and eating the last of their bread just as it was growing dark.

"We must find somewhere to shelter," Olivia said, looking up at the sky, which was clouding over.

"There Is farm over there, perhaps there is a barn where we can hide for the night and sleep amidst the straw?" Mabel Marie said, and the two of them hurried off the lane and over a field, to where the outline of farm buildings could be seen in the gathering gloom.

There seemed to be no one about, a solitary lamp burning in a window of the farmhouse, and the two girls slipped into one barn, closing the door behind them.

"Oh, what is this?" Olivia said, as she stumbled into a pile of hard little balls.

But Mabel Marie laughed. "Can you not tell? They are apples, I can smell them, thank goodness, we shall have a feast," she said, and Olivia heard the crunch as she bit into one.

The apples were delicious, windfalls stored for cider, perhaps, and soon the two girls had eaten their fill. With much groping about in the darkness, they discovered the barn ran back to where a ladder went up to a hayloft above. There were no animals there, though they could hear cattle in some distant field. The hay made a comfortable bed, and they were soon settling down to sleep, lying together for warmth.

"Do you think Mrs. Dounce has discovered we are missing?" Mabel Marie asked, yawning, and rolling onto her side.

"I do not think they will discover it until the morning, and then it will be too late. She will notice when we are not at our benches in the workshop," Olivia replied.

"By which time we will walk the streets of London, paved with gold," Mabel Marie replied.

"We still have a long way to go," Olivia said, for she knew London lay some fifty miles away from the orphanage, and she was not even certain that they were going in the right direction.

"Paved with gold," Mabel Marie repeated, and Olivia listened as she fell asleep, snoring gently in the hay.

She herself remained awake for some time, listening to the unfamiliar sounds of the countryside, until finally she drifted into a dreamless sleep. An owl hooted in the rafters of the barn and down below mice scuttled over the apple piles, as outside the cattle lowed. But it was the cockerel which awoke her, its call echoing over the farm, just as the first rays of dawn poured through the wooden slats in the barn door.

Olivia rolled over, and for a moment she was uncertain of where she was, rubbing her eyes and sitting up. Mabel Marie was still fast asleep, lying curled up in the hay and looking ever so peaceful. Olivia could now hear voices outside, and she shrank back fearfully, listening lest they had been discovered.

But it was only the farmer and his farmhands, the older man calling out orders for the day, chief amongst them to milk the cows and see to the eggs from the hens. Olivia shook Mabel Marie away, and she sat up, looking around her in surprise, just as Olivia had done when she awoke.

"Oh, I was having the most wonderful dream. Mrs. Dounce was being chased by a giant apple, and it ate her up. Mr. Dounce was ever so cross, but then the apple chased him too," she said, and Olivia laughed.

"Well, come now, we should eat some apples and be on our way," she said, and she stood up, jumping down into the barn below.

But as she stood and turned around, a sight before her caused her to let out a cry. She had not heard the barn door open, nor seen the young farmhand who now stood before her. He seemed just as surprised to see her, even more so when Mabel Marie dropped next to her.

"Here, who are you? What do you want?" he asked, as Olivia and Mabel Marie both tried to make their excuses.

"We are sorry, sir. We needed somewhere to sleep. We will be on our way, please say nothing to anyone," Olivia said.

"Oh, please, please do not hand us over," Mabel Marie begged, and the young farmhand scratched his head and smiled.

"Hand you over? Well, who am I to hand you over to? Are you running away from something?" he said, furrowing his brow.

"We … no, we are just trying to get to London," Olivia said, knowing that it was best to say as little as possible about where they had come from.

"To London? Well, I see. And what do two little girls like you want to go to London for?" he asked.

"The gold-paved streets," Mabel Marie said, her voice sounding ever so authoritative and determined.

"Well, I do not know about any gold-paved streets, but you will find London a big place for two such as you who cannot even hide in a barn without being discovered," he said, smiling and shaking his head.

"Please do not tell anyone about us. We only slept here," Olivia said, and the farmhand raised his eyebrow.

"And ate a few of my father's apples too, I see," he said, pointing to a pile of apple cores on the barn floor.

"Oh, but we were hungry," Mabel Marie said, and the farmhand laughed.

"We have more apples than we know what to do with. A man can only drink so much cider and eat so much apple pie. Go on, be off with you, and take a few for your journey. You can have a drink from the water pump out in the yard. My father is away with the cattle now, so you will not be seen," he said, and Olivia and Mabel Marie thanked him profusely.

"Is this the right way to London?" Olivia asked, after they had taken a long drink from the water pump.

"Go down this lane where the trees arch over and then out onto the road there, turn right and you shall soon see a milestone for London. Good luck to you, I hope you find your gold," he said, and waved them off, as Olivia and Mabel Marie ran off along the lane.

"I thought he was going to take us back to Mr. and Mrs. Dounce," Mabel Marie said, as they walked beneath the trees and out onto the road the farmhand had pointed them to.

"Not everyone in this world is bad," Olivia said, and Mabel Marie smiled.

"I am sure my mother is not. She will look after us, we will find her and she will take care of us," Mabel Marie said, taking Olivia by the hand.

But Olivia was not so sure. She knew little of London, but she was certain it was a far bigger place than Mabel Marie believed it to be. Surely, they would not find her mother so easily, and even if they did, would she really wish anything to do with them? The thought made Olivia think of her own story, and she wondered if she herself had come from London, just like her friend.

"Then we had best hurry, here, look, the milestone says forty miles," Olivia said, pointing to the white marker at the edge of the road.

"Then we will be there in a few days," Mabel Marie said, and the two of them set off arm in arm, their adventures only just beginning.

Chapter 4
Where is the Gold?

The two girls walked on for much of the day, eating the apples they had brought with them from the farm, and drinking from streams and wells along the way. Whenever they heard horses or a mail coach along the road, they hid, fearful lest Mr. Dounce or one of his men ride by on the hunt for them.

But any search which the Dounce's had mounted was in vain, and they spent another night in a farmer's barn, cautious to avoid encountering anyone by leaving early in the morning. In this way, following the road and sleeping where they could find shelter, they came at last in sight of London, the dome of Saint Paul's rising above the river some miles further on. It was four days since they had left the orphanage and the sight of their objective brought fresh heart to their weary bodies.

"Look, there is Saint Paul's, I remember Mr. Dounce talking of attending matins there when he was in London on business," Mabel Marie said, pointing to where the dome could be seen above the roofs of houses which cascaded down toward the riverbanks.

Olivia could not believe her eyes at the sight of the magnificent church. It grew ever bigger as they approached, the sound of its bells now echoing out across the marshland where they walked. Soon, they came to where the first houses clung to the river's edge, where women stood waist deep in the waters washing clothes and children played upon the banks.

"Where do we go now?" Olivia asked, and Mabel Marie looked at her and shrugged.

"I … I do not know," she said, looking around her, as though she expected the rough road to have changed to a pavement of gold.

"Ah, 'London one mile,' look, it says so on this milestone," Olivia said, and Mabel Marie smiled.

"Then that is where the golden pavement begins. Come along, we must get there before the afternoon draws on," she said, hurrying off along the road, which led over a bridge to the other side of the river.

There, it wound its way past houses, shops, and churches, where hundreds of people milled about, calling to one another and trading wares.

"Milk, milk for sale, penny a quart, fresh milk from the farm," one man called out, two buckets hanging from a spoke across his back.

"Fish, fresh fish, all manner of fish," another called out.

"Flowers, fresh flowers for the ladies. Will you buy a flower, sir?" a woman called out, and Olivia and Mabel Marie looked about them in astonishment.

They had never seen so many people, nor been part of such a crowd. The noise was almost deafening, as horses clip-clopped past, drawing hansom cabs, and shouts came from every which way and direction. Many smells filled the air, freshly baking bread, roasting meat, and the stench of the river and the filth lying in the streets, all combined, so that Olivia and Mabel Marie could only clutch at one another in astonishment, overwhelmed by all that was around them.

"Whitechapel murders; read the details, Whitechapel murders," a boy selling newspapers called out.

"Fortune telling, have your fortune read," an old, wizened woman called out, and Olivia and Mabel Marie backed away as she approached.

"Now, children, there is nothing to be afraid of. Come to me, you shall be safe here," a man said, leering out of the door of a barber's shop and beckoning them inside.

Olivia and Mabel Marie ran, pushing through the crowds, and only stopping when they could go no further through exhaustion, panting and breathless.

"Where is the gold?" Mabel Marie asked.

"I do not see it, but there is Saint Paul's. Look, we are below the dome now," Olivia said, pointing up to where the cathedral rose majestically into the skies.

"Then this is London," Mabel Marie said, sounding heartbroken, as she gazed around her in search of the promised golden pavement.

But the streets were only muddy, covered in filth and rubbish, a foul stench filling the air all around them.

"It is not as I expected it to be," Olivia said, and Mabel Marie shook her head.

"I am hungry. Where can we get food?" she said, the two of them having eaten the last of their apples along the way.

"We have no money, and if we steal, then we shall surely be caught. We will have to beg," Olivia said, suddenly wondering if they had been right to leave the orphanage behind.

At least there they had had a roof over their heads, something to eat and shelter from the weather. Now, it was raining, the mud in the streets churning up, no one paying any attention to two little girls who huddled in the cathedral's doorway.

"Please, sir, can you spare any money?" Mabel Marie asked, as a man hurried by, "we are starving, please, anyone."

But no one gave them a second glance, the rain now falling heavily, as the clouds swirled gloomily around the domes of Saint Paul's and the attraction of London seemed far from that which they had dreamed.

"Look, there is a policeman over there," Olivia said, when they had stood in the cathedral's doorway for around half an hour.

The bell had just tolled three o'clock, the rain ceasing, though everywhere was now wet and muddy. Olivia and Mabel Marie took one another by the hand and hurried over to where the policeman was walking stiffly upon his patrol. He did not see them at first, and it was only when Mabel Marie tugged at his tunic that he looked down.

"Yes?" he said, eyeing them suspiciously.

"Have you seen my mother?" Mabel Marie asked, and the policeman glared at her.

"Your mother? What nonsense. What makes you think I would have seen your mother? Is she like you? A beggar? There are a thousand beggars in this city, be off with you," he said, and Mabel Marie cried.

"Please, sir, where is the gold pavement?" Olivia asked, and now the policeman tutted and pushed them both roughly away.

"Gold pavement? I will give you gold pavement, my girl. What nonsense. There is no gold pavement, only a brass key turned in the debtor's prison lock for the likes of urchins like you. Now, be gone," he said, and strode off shaking his head and muttering about unruly beggars and the consequences they should face.

"I do not think we will find the help we thought we would," Olivia said, and Mabel Marie shook her head.

"I am sorry, Olivia. I should not have brought you here," she said, and a tear ran down her cheek.

"You were not to know. Besides, we would only have dreamed of it. If we had not left, then we would always have thought of doing so," Olivia said, trying to find some hope in the tragedy of their current situation.

"But what are we to eat? Where are we to go? Back out into the countryside? But then what?" Mabel Marie said.

Olivia shook her head. She did not know what they were to do or where they were to go. She sighed, looking around just as a woman approached them. The woman was well dressed, wearing a sash over her petticoat and a hat with flowers and fruits woven into it. She smiled at them, stooping down, and putting her hand upon Olivia's shoulder.

"You poor dears, are you out here all alone?" she asked, and Olivia shook her head.

"No … our mother has sent us … out … to buy bread, but we lost the penny she gave us, and we dare not go back home empty handed," she said.

The woman smiled, evidently willing to believe her story, and she smiled at them again.

"Myself and several other ladies try to do what good we can with the poor around Saint Paul's. We have a little food to give, some money too, if it would help. Tell your mother to come and see us here," she said, and pointed over to where a group of similarly dressed ladies were handing out parcels of food to a line of the city's poor.

"Please, ma'am, our mother is sick," Mabel Marie said, "and that is why we must buy bread for her."

"Oh, dear, how terrible. Come then, you shall have a parcel to take to her, and if you tell me where you live then I shall ensure that our relief fund comes to visit you," she said, hurrying over to the other women and returning with a parcel of food.

"You are ever so kind, miss," Mabel Marie said.

"It is our Christian duty," the woman said, handing Olivia the parcel, "and your address?"

Olivia and Mabel Marie looked at one another.

"Er … thirteen … Dounce Street," Olivia said, and Mabel Marie almost burst out laughing.

"Dounce Street, ah, yes, I think I know it," the lady said, and patted them both upon the head, "do not worry, life will be better soon, I promise you."

Olivia and Mabel Marie thanked the woman once again, before hurrying off along the street which ran parallel to the cathedral, not stopping until they were well away from the woman and her charitable guild.

"I cannot believe we got away with that," Olivia said, embarrassed at the thought of the lie she had told.

"We have to eat," Mabel Marie replied, and Olivia nodded.

"I know, but …" Olivia began, but she cut her words short with the appearance of two older boys, scruffy and dishevelled, who attempted to snatch the parcel from her hands.

"Give that back," she cried out, clinging to the food parcel, as Mabel Marie pushed the other boy away.

"Give us, we want it, give us," he said, as Olivia let out a cry.

Mabel Marie now kicked the boy who was struggling with Olivia and he fell back into the mud, the two girls now running off along the street, the two boys pursuing behind.

"This way," Mabel Marie said, and she darted into a side alleyway, as Olivia almost dropped the food parcel.

"But this way leads nowhere," Olivia said, as they came to a dead end, dog barking viciously from a doorway, a high wall preventing any further escape.

"You will be sorry for this," the first of the two boys said, advancing toward them.

Both Olivia and Mabel Marie were brave, but they would be no match for the two boys who had now rolled up their sleeves and were preparing to fight.

"All right, you can have it," Olivia said, holding out the box, as tears welled up in her eyes.

"Have it, take it, it is all the same to us," the second boy said, and lunged forward to snatch the box from Olivia's hand.

But as he did so, he let out a cry and stumbled back. A pellet or some other object had hit him squarely between the eyes and he staggered, just as a shout from behind caused the two boys to turn.

"You leave them alone," a boy shouted, and suddenly three others ran up behind him.

"Gobler's boys, quick, come on," the boy who had been hit by the projectile shouted, and the two boys ran off, dropping the food parcel as they went.

Olivia and Mabel Marie clutched at one another, terrified at what would happen next. Two assailants had now been replaced by four, the boys now hurrying toward them, and a dead end behind. They were each around ten years old, dressed in an odd assortment of clothes, none of which fitted. The leader was holding a catapult and wore an ill-fitting top hat and blue breeches. He cocked his head and looked at them, before the four all unexpectedly bowed.

"Marvo Tomkins, at your service," he said, grinning at them to reveal a toothless smile.

"Olivia, and this is Mabel Marie," Olivia said, still wary as to what the intention of these strangely dressed boys really was.

"And this is Wisbottle, O'Bleary, and Beadle," Tomkins said, and the other three bowed again.

They each wore peaked hats and long coats, which trailed upon the ground.

"You had a lucky escape from the Boxer twins, if we had not come along then they would have had your parcel of food there and whatever else you are carrying," Wisbottle said, tutting and shaking his head.

"And I suppose you shall have them now," Olivia said, and Tomkins shook his head.

"Do you hear that, gentleman? The lady thinks that we shall have her food and be off with it. A thankful response to being rescued," he said, and Olivia blushed.

"Very thankful, Tomkins. We saved them, we did," O'Bleary said.

"Saved them from far worse than us," Beadle replied, and the four boys nodded to one another.

"Then what do you want with us?" Olivia asked.

"Well, it seems to me that you are unfamiliar with London town, am I right?" Tomkins asked, his broad cockney accent sounding almost comical to Olivia, who was used to the gentle country tones of the orphanage neighbours.

"If this is London, then where is the gold?" Mabel Marie asked, and Tomkins laughed.

"Ah, so you are one of those, I see. Yes, escaped from somewhere, have we? Runaways?" he said, and the others nodded.

"Yes, runaways. Mr. Gobler could use runaways," Wisbottle said.

"We … we came here to find someone," Olivia said, glancing at Mabel Marie.

"Do you know my mother?" she asked, and Tomkins laughed.

"We do not even know our own mothers, let alone yours, miss. But we know a place where you could lodge, a warm place, with food and company," he said.

"Our company," O'Bleary interjected.

"Oh, excellent company, and Mr. Gobler is a charming man, an excellent man," Beadle said.

"We will be all right, thank you," Olivia said, but Tomkins shook his head.

"And what happens when the Boxer twins return, and we are not here to defend you? These streets are not safe," he said, and the others nodded once more.

"Not safe at all. Not safe for two little girls. But Mr. Gobler is a kindly gent, he will look after you, just as he looks after us all," Wisbottle said.

"We do not want to go to an orphanage," Olivia said, and Tomkins laughed.

"An orphanage? Oh, bless me soul, so that is where you two have run away from, is it? This is no orphanage," he said.

"More … a lodging house, though you will pay nothing to lodge there. Once Mr. Gobler trusts you, that is …" Beadle said, and the others laughed.

"Oh yes, Mr, Gobler must trust you. But come now, we have enough food to go around, a warm bed. See, the sky is darkening, and the streets become far worse at night. No place for girls like you," Tomkins said, shaking his head.

"No place at all," Wisbottle said, and the other agreed.

Olivia looked at Mabel Marie. The thought of a hot meal and a warm bed was attractive, and the four boys *had* saved them from a far worse fate.

"And we will pay nothing?" she asked, and Tomkins shook his head.

"Not a farthing, though Mr. Gobler expects you to pull your weight a bit, do your chores, and so on. We all help," he said.

"Oh, we all help as best we can," Beadle said.

"Very well, we will come with you," Olivia said, and Tomkins smiled.

"An excellent choice, madam. Now, if you will take my arm, we shall escort you to Mr. Gobler's lodgings, a finer place in all this great city you will not find," he said, as Olivia and Mabel Marie now followed the four boys through the darkening streets.

There was no gold paving them, but perhaps now there was more than just a little hope.

Chapter 5
Mr. Artemis Gobler

Olivia and Mabel Marie followed the four boys through the darkening streets, holding hands and looking nervously around them. It was true what Tomkins had said, for London appeared foreboding as the moon rose, the gas lamps lit, and the shadows murky and threatening. Olivia did not like it and she could sense the fear in Mabel Marie, who clung tightly to her hand, the six of them walking for what seemed like miles.

"Where are we going?" Olivia asked, and Wisbottle turned to her with a smile.

"To Camden, Miss Olivia, Camden Town. See, we are here now," he said, raising his hand, as though he were showing her some marvellous spectacle.

The surrounding buildings seemed no different, if anything they were more foreboding, large tenements and rows of slum houses stretching out in every direction. The air was thick with smog and the sounds of labour, even at this late hour, echoed all around. They dodged past beggars and pedlars, and Olivia let out a cry as an old, wizened man leered out at them from a doorway and tried to grab hold of Mabel Marie.

"Help!" she cried, and the four boys turned and laughed.

"It is only old William. He just wants to say good evening to you, Miss Mabel Marie. Come on, we are nearly at the gentleman's lodgings," Beadle said, and suddenly they turned down a side street, quiet and deserted.

Olivia could see the street sign illuminated by a gas lamp, though she could not read what it said, and she pointed up to it as the four boys hurried to a doorway built under an arch to their right.

"Where are we?" she asked, and Tomkins smiled.

"Moon Street, Miss Olivia, the home of Mr. Artemis Gobler and now your home too," he said, ushering them through the door.

It emerged into a shadowy yard, lit now only by the faint moonlight coming through the hanging smog. Olivia could make out a flight of rickety wooden steps leading up to a walkway above and another archway beyond, high walls surrounding them on either side. There was a strong smell of rotting meat in the air, which made her hold a hand to her nose, feeling as though she would be sick at any moment.

"That abattoir, Miss Olivia, the yard backs onto it, but you get used to the smell," Wisbottle said, and Tomkins led them up the steps and along the walkway to a door, from behind which there came much noise and commotion.

"Welcome to the home of Mr. Artemis Gobler and associates," Tomkins said, a note of pride in his voice, as he pushed open the door.

Olivia and Mabel Marie followed nervously behind, and what they now saw was a most astonishing sight. Through the door, a long attic room ran the length of what must have been a warehouse below. At the far end, a merry fire burned in a hearth and around a dozen children sat along a trestle table eating a fine array of food, including roasted meats, raised pies, pastries, and many delights the likes of which Olivia had only ever seen on the table of the Dounces.

Along each wall there ran a series of bunk beds built into the eaves and alcoves, and worn old armchairs surrounded the fireplace. But it was the figure at the head of the table which drew Olivia's eye. An old man with a long white beard and a smoking cap upon his head. He had a pipe in his mouth, with a long stem, from which he was blowing smoke rings, much to the delight of the surrounding children.

As the door opened, he looked up and smiled, rising to his feet, and stepping forward. The rest of the room fell silent, and Tomkins pushed Olivia and Mabel Marie forward so that the gentleman could see them. He cocked his head to one side, narrowing his eyes, before his face lit up in a most delightful smile. Olivia did not know whether to fear him or pleased to meet him, and she could only wonder what sort of place this was. An orphanage? But one quite unlike that of Craddock's Correction House.

"My dears," the man said, his voice sounding somewhat foreign, "my dears, what have we here? Who have we here?" and he hurried forward, looking Olivia and Mabel Marie up and down with interest, before turning to Tomkins.

"These two young ladies, Miss Olivia and Miss Mabel Marie were about to meet a nasty end at the hands of the Boxer twins, Mr. Gobler, and so we considered it our civic duty to protect them," Tomkins said, and the other three boys nodded.

"Civic duty, Mr. Gobler," O'Bleary said.

"Well now, those Boxer twins, well, well, well. You had a lucky escape, my dears, a lucky escape. How fortunate to have come across my boys as you did," Mr. Gobler said, running his tongue over his teeth.

"Please, sir, we have come to London in search of gold," Mabel Marie said, her hand still clasped in Olivia's.

"Gold?" Mr. Gobler said, and he laughed, turning to the other children, "did you hear that, my dears? They have come here looking for gold," and the other children laughed.

"They will find gold all right, Mr. Gobler, sir," Tomkins said, and the gentleman nodded.

"Indeed, they will, indeed they will. Well, my little gold seekers, you are most welcome here, most welcome. Come and sit yourselves down and tell me all about yourselves," he said, pointing to the head of the table where two chairs had been drawn up on either side of him.

"We may eat?" Olivia asked, looking hungrily at the food laid out upon the table, a feast such as she had never dared dream of.

"Eat? Of course you may eat. Eat your fill, drink your fill, and eat some more," Mr. Gobler said, ushering them to the table.

Tomkins, Wisbottle, O'Bleary, and Beadle took their places too, and soon the room was once more filled with merry laughter and conversation. Olivia and Mabel Marie sat, one on either side of Artemis, who cut them generous portions of a large meat pie and bid them to eat.

"We have no money to pay though, sir," Olivia said, looking longingly at the food.

"Pay? Does a guest pay for his meal? No, my dears, you must eat, for it is clear you have come a long way to join the feast. But in return, you will tell me your story from the beginning," he said, pulling the leg from a chicken and gnawing it.

Olivia took a large bite of the pie. It was the most delicious thing she had ever tasted, the pastry rich and buttery, the meat succulent and full of flavour. After the years of gruel and stale bread she had endured at the hands of the Dounces, this was a feast to surpass all others.

"Well, sir," she began, "I do not remember my mother and father or where I came from, but ever since I can remember I have lived, along with my closest friend here, Mabel Marie, at Craddock's Correction House ..." and so she told their story.

Mr. Gobler listened with interest, interjecting with questions along the way and nodding when he heard a familiar name or place.

"Oh yes, I have heard of the Dounces and of Craddock's Correction House," he said as Olivia concluded her tale.

"You will not send us back there though, will you, sir?" Olivia said, horrified for a moment that she had said too much.

"Send you back? Goodness me no, my dear. I would send no child to such a terrible place. I am a charitable man myself and I make it my business to take care of those, like you, who have fallen on hard times. Is that not right, boys?" Mr. Gobler said, and the other children nodded.

"The very best care, Mr. Gobler," Tomkins said, chewing on a large piece of pie.

"Mind your manners, Tomkins, do not speak with your mouth full, not when ladies are present," Mr. Gobler said, smiling at the boy who grinned back.

Olivia now noticed that she and Mabel Marie were the only girls at the table, and she looked round curiously, wondering why that was so.

"You have only boys here, sir," she said, and Mr. Gobler nodded.

"Because few girls have your courage, Miss Olivia. It is rare that a girl needs my help. Boys are always running away and getting into mischief, but girls, well they stay with their mothers or enter domestic service. All very nice, I am sure. But would you not rather live a life like this?" he said, pointing along the table, to where more things had been laid out to eat.

"But what do you do here?" Olivia asked, for it still confused her what sort of place this was.

"You shall see soon enough, but for now you must rest, my dear. Tomorrow you will learn more," he said, smiling at her.

They finished the meal and one by one, the other children drifted off to their bunk beds. Candles burned around the room, and Olivia was astonished that none of the children were asked to wash or say their prayers. If this was an orphanage, then it was a strange one indeed. Artemis had retired to an armchair by the fire and was wreathed in clouds of tobacco smoke, which smelt fragrant in the air.

"I like it here," Mabel Marie whispered, and Olivia nodded.

"I do too, but I do not understand it," she said.

"They are kind," Mabel Marie replied, and Olivia could only agree.

"Oh, my dears, you will want somewhere to sleep, how rude of me," Mr. Gobler said, springing up from his armchair.

He stepped to one side of the chimney breast and pulled back a thick curtain, behind which were two empty bunk beds, as though prepared just upon the off chance of visitors. Mr. Gobler handed them each a candle and ushered them toward the beds.

"Our own little bedroom," Mabel Marie said, her voice filled with awe.

"I would have it no other way, my dear," Mr. Gobler said.

"And we may sleep here?" Olivia asked, and he laughed.

"My dear, you are no longer an orphan, you have a family now. You may sleep and eat and be merry. That is what I want for all my boys—and my girls now," he said, and with a flourish and a bow, he bid them goodnight.

Mabel Marie took the top bunk and Olivia the bottom, and Olivia snuffed out her candle as she pulled the blankets over her. She felt warm and safe, her stomach full and her mind filled with many thoughts and questions. What a strange place this was and what a kindly man they had found in Artemis Gobler. Fortune had come their way, and as she drifted to sleep, Olivia wondered if perhaps the streets of London were paved with gold, only a gold quite different to that which she had imagined.

***

"Olivia, wake up, wake up, we are to have bacon and eggs," Mabel Marie's excited voice said, as Olivia opened her eyes and yawned.

The smell of cooking was wafting across the attic, and the sound of voices echoed all around. She sat up and smiled, the look on Mabel Marie's face like one who has received the most fortuitous news.

"Bacon?" she said, rubbing her eyes.

"I have only ever smelt it cooking when the Dounce's had breakfast, but Mr. Gobler is cooking it for us. He says we are to have two eggs each," Mabel Marie said, and just then, the curtain was pulled back and Tomkins' grinning face appeared in front of them.

"Hurry, ladies, come and sit down, we have a busy day ahead of us," he said, beckoning them to follow him.

Olivia and Mabel Marie hurriedly made their way out into the attic where Mr. Gobler was bent over the fire. An enormous hissing, spitting frying pan sat over the flames. He looked up at them and smiled, a gold tooth sparkling in his mouth.

"Good morning, my dear Miss Olivia. I trust you slept well. Miss Mabel Marie was awake early and has been a great help to me. Come now, sit yourself down," he said, and brought the pan of bacon and eggs to the table.

Olivia had never tasted bacon either, not to mention eating eggs on only the rarest of occasions at Christmas and Easter. But this breakfast appeared entirely normal, the other children all sitting down expectantly. Olivia and Mabel Marie joined them, sitting patiently and waiting for the grace.

"Help yourself, Miss Olivia, or it will be all gone," Beadle said, and Olivia glanced at Mr. Gobler in confusion.

"Do we not say Grace, Mr Gobler?" she asked, and the old gentleman smiled.

"Forgive me, Miss Olivia, where are my manners. Boys!" he shouted, "wait a moment, for now that we have ladies present it is only right that we say grace before our meals. Miss Olivia, if you will, please," and he made a point of putting his hands together and bowing his head.

The room fell silent, though there was some sniggering amongst the younger boys and Olivia cleared her throat, suddenly feeling terribly nervous.

"May … may the Lord make us thankful for this bounty he has set before us and let us always be mindful of others with less," she said.

"Amen," Mr. Gobler replied, "and may we all enjoy the fruits of our labours," and he laughed, as did the others.

"Can we eat now, Mr. Gobler?" Wisbottle asked, reaching out to help himself from the frying pan.

"You must forgive my boys, Miss Olivia. They are not used to having ladies present. Allow Miss Olivia and Miss Mabel Marie to be served first, Wisbottle," he said, and turning to Olivia with a smile, he offered her an egg, insisting that she take two.

When they finished breakfast, and Olivia and Mabel Marie agreed it was the most delicious breakfast they had ever eaten, the children all lined up at the end of the room. Olivia and Mabel Marie watched with interest as Mr. Gobler stepped forward like a Sergeant Major making an inspection.

"Now, boys, it is very important that you remember what I tell you every day," Mr. Gobler said, and a chorus came in response.

"Watch your back and do not get caught," the children said in unison.

"And when has that rule ever let you down?" Mr. Gobler asked.

"Never," came the reply, and the old man smiled.

"Never. That is right. Now, Lewis and Finch, you take Kentish Town, Fizzler and Bonce you go to the City and Saint Paul's, Gozo and Puglisi you take Canning Town. Hoskin and Pippin, you stay here and help me," he said, and the children all nodded.

"What about us, Mr. Gobler, sir?" Tomkins said.

"I have a very special task for the four of you," he replied, turning to Olivia and Mabel Marie, whom he beckoned forward with a smile.

"Please, sir. What are we to do?" Olivia asked, and Mr. Gobler ran his tongue over his teeth and grinned.

"Tomkins and my other best boys will see you two learn our ways and quickly," he said, and the other children laughed.

"Ways, sir?" Olivia asked, glancing at Mabel Marie.

"Yes, my dear, our ways. You do not think all of this comes from nothing, do you? Go with Tomkins and the others. They will show you," Mr. Gobler said, and he ushered them forward.

"I do not understand," Mabel Marie whispered, but Olivia thought she now did, and it was with a heavy heart that she followed Tomkins, Wisbottle, O'Bleary, and Beadle out of the door, as Mr. Gobler called encouragingly after them.

"Cheerio, my dears, be back soon and be sure to bring plenty with you. They line the streets of London with gold, if only you know where to look. I shall wait for you when you return. God bless you, my dear children, and remember what I said, watch your backs and do not get caught," he called out.

Olivia and Mabel Marie followed Tomkins and the others out of the door and along the rickety walkway and down the wooden steps into the yard of the abattoir. The rancid smell still hung in the air and there were shouts and cries from all around, carcasses slung up and the gates out onto the street now wide open.

Camden Town was alive with the hustle and bustle of the city, carriages and hansom cabs driving up and down, men and women plying their trades and the shops and businesses opening for trade. Mabel Marie took hold of Olivia's hand, the two of them following nervously after Tomkins, the four boys weaving and winding their way through the crowds until they came to the front of a large bank, with colonnades stretching up to an archway above and well-dressed ladies and gentleman hurrying in and out.

"Today, Miss Olivia, Miss Mabel Marie, you are to learn the noble art of the pickpocket, as practiced by generations of our noble predecessors," Tomkins said, sounding for all the world as though what he was suggesting was something to be proud of.

Olivia could hear Mr. Houlding in one of his sermons condemning theft as a sin against God, and she glanced at Mabel Marie, who was looking at Tomkins in astonishment.

"You steal?" she asked, her eyes wide and questioning.

"We only steal from those who can afford it, Miss Mabel Marie," Tomkins said, placing his thumbs into the lapels of his waistcoat, as though he were preparing to deliver an important lecture.

"But you take those things that do not belong to you?" Olivia asked, and the other three boys laughed.

"Allow Tomkins to explain, Miss Olivia," Beadle said, and Tomkins nodded.

"There are those in this world," he began, clearing his throat, "there are those in this world who have and those who have not. Now, you yourself have experienced having not and the injustice that arises from seeing those who have lauded it over you. Think of the orphanage governors. Did they weep over giving you gruel and stale bread when they themselves sat down to bacon and eggs, Miss Olivia? I think not."

"Well, no, but …" Olivia replied, still thinking of the curate's sermons, which promised fire and damnation for those who broke the sacred commandments.

"Then I put it to you, Miss Olivia, that if a man has too much for himself, is it not our right, nay, our duty, to take it from him and give it to those who have not?" Tomkins said, and the other boys nodded in agreement.

"Perfectly right," Wisbottle said.

"Our duty," Beadle said, and O'Blear nodded.

"Pick-pocketing is not theft, Miss Olivia. We take only from those who can afford and spread it out amongst those with nothing, which would be us. There is a kindly gentleman living up in Highgate, a friend of Mr. Gobler's, a man called Mr. Karl Marx, and he thinks just the same as we do. He even wrote a book about it. Take from the rich and give to the poor," Tomkins said, and he grinned at them, as Olivia glanced nervously at Mabel Marie.

"And we are to steal?" Olivia asked, and the four boys laughed.

"Mr. Gobler would not allow that, not at first, no. Remember what he said. Watch your backs and do not get caught. We are the professionals, Miss Olivia, and for now, you are to watch us and see what we do," Tomkins replied.

"And here is just the gentleman," Beadle said, nodding his head to where a well-dressed gentleman was counting notes from a pocketbook, having just emerged from the bank.

"But what do we do?" Olivia asked, terrified by the prospect of stealing, however it might be justified.

"We follow him. Come along," Tomkins said, and the four boys darted off in pursuit of their quarry.

Olivia and Mabel Marie had no choice but to follow behind, the gentleman making his way up the broad high street toward Kentish Town.

"I dislike it, Olivia," Mabel Marie said, and Olivia shook her head.

"Neither do I, but what choice do we have? We cannot live on the streets. Stay close now, let us see what happens," she said, and they hurried on behind until Tomkins and the others paused round a corner, outside a bookseller, around half a mile from the bank.

"Now is the perfect time, you go, Wisbottle," he said, and Olivia and Mabel Marie watched in amazement as Wisbottle sauntered up to the man and stood at his side, making a pretence of examining the books.

"I think Mr. Dickens is very fine, do you not, sir?" he asked, and the gentleman looked down at him in surprise.

"Oh, well, yes, I do. Although that is a novel by Mr. Trollope," the man replied, and Wisbottle grinned.

"I always confuse them, sir," he said, as Beadle crept forward.

Olivia held her breath as Wisbottle continued to talk to the man, questioning him as to the books he was buying, whilst O'Bleary raised the tail of his frock coat and deftly withdrew the pocketbook they had seen him counting notes into outside the bank.

"Well, sir, it has been a delight to speak with you on matters of literature. I had best be running on now, or my mother will wonder where I am," Wisbottle said.

"What a fine young man, here, a shilling for your trouble," the man said, and he reached into his pocket and brought out a shiny shilling, which he handed to Wisbottle with a smile.

O'Bleary was now hurrying along the other side of the street and with the gentleman now making his way inside the bookseller's, the other children ran off into the crowd, meeting together outside a butcher's shop some way further on.

"Look at all this," O'Bleary said, as he opened the pocketbook to reveal more money than Olivia had ever imagined in all her life.

"And meat pies all round with this shilling," Wisbottle said, and he hurried into the butcher's shop, returning a moment later with six large pies, still hot from the oven.

"And that, Miss Olivia, Miss Mabel Marie, is the honourable art of the pickpocket," Tomkins said, smiling at them proudly.

"But … is it not wrong?" she said, and the four boys shook their heads.

"Will that gentleman sit down to a hearty dinner tonight? Will he sleep in a warm bed with maids and cooks and footmen to see to his every need? Yes, he will. And will he miss a few pounds from his pocketbook in a year's time? No, he will not. But this money will see us fed for weeks and fuel for the fire for a month. Mr. Gobler will be pleased, very pleased," Tomkins replied.

"Or would you prefer to go back to the alleyway behind Saint Paul's and chance your luck with the Boxer twins?" Beadle asked, the four boys now fixing Olivia and Mabel Marie with a questioning look.

Olivia glanced at Mabel Marie, the two of them nodding, for it was clear they had no choice.

"We understand," Olivia said, and Tomkins smiled.

"Of course you do, you are one of us now," he said, and the four boys ran off into the crowds, followed by Olivia and Mabel Marie, who knew that their lives were now to be very different to what once they had been.

Chapter 6
The Art of the Pickpocket

When they returned to the attic above the warehouse, the children found Artemis stirring a large pot of stew over the fire. Their offerings impressed him, for they had robbed two further gentlemen of their pocketbooks, along with taking a side of ham and a crate of apples from the back of a grocer's shop on the high street.

"Very good, my dears, very good, and now Miss Olivia, Miss Mabel Marie, you know our noble business," he said, counting the notes out of the pocketbooks and licking his lips.

"Is it ... is it right?" Olivia asked, and Mr. Gobler raised his eyebrow to her.

"Has Tomkins not explained, my dear? Of course it is right, Mr. Marx says so. To take from those who have and give to those who have not is a noble thing. We are not common thieves who steal from those with nothing," he said, drawing himself up, as though her comments had offended him.

Olivia did not wish to upset the old gentleman, for he had been exceptionally kind to them, and without his hospitality they would still be scared and alone upon the dangerous streets of London.

"I did not mean to cause offence," she said, and he laughed.

"There is none taken, my dear. I force no one to do my work for me, but I hope very much that you will stay?" he said, and Olivia nodded.

"We have nowhere else to go," she replied, and Artemis smiled.

"Then it is agreed. Tomkins and the others will soon teach you all they know. Besides, people trust girls, girls can go places where boys cannot. I think you will become very useful, my dears, very useful indeed," he said, just as there came a hammering at the door.

It burst open to reveal a large and thick set man wearing a scruffy top hat and a blue frock coat, splattered with mud. His breeches were dirty, and he held a sack in his hand, which he threw down upon the floor, a dog yapping at his heels.

"Gobler, I have what you wanted, now pay me," he growled, as the children crowded round him, as though this were the visit of a favourite uncle.

"Ah, Cymon, come in, come in," Mr. Gobler said, stepping forward.

"New blood?" the man said, pointing to Olivia and Mabel Marie.

"Yes, indeed, Miss Olivia and Miss Mabel Marie, may I introduce you to our dear friend My. Cymon Tuggs," Mr. Gobler said, and the man nodded to them.

"Small hands, good for thieving," he said, looking down at the hand which Olivia had now held out to him.

She had never known her superiors to speak with her on such familiar terms. Mr. Gobler appeared to treat all the children as though they were his own, and there was no sense of fear or trepidation in their eyes, only unwavering loyalty.

"Mr. Tuggs is a professional," Mr. Gobler said, and the man laughed.

He was young, perhaps in his twenties, with a scar running almost the full length of his neck. His hands were grubby, and he appeared dishevelled, but there was a quickness to him, an alertness, as though he were used to finding himself in tight situations, always poised to fight or run.

"We shall see what the two of you can do, soon enough. Now, Gobler, where is my money? I am to go to the Monkey and Barrel tonight and I want rum and ale, lots of it," he said, holding out his hand.

Mr. Gobler turned his back away and Olivia watched as he counted out five notes from the stole pocketbooks, before turning to Cymon and bowing.

"As we agreed. Is it all there?" he said, and Cymon nodded.

"Along with a string of pearls his wife had left on her dressing table," Cymon said, counting the money and putting it into his pocket.

"Pearls? Oh, very nice, my dear, very nice," Mr. Gobler said, and Olivia watched in astonishment as Tomkins opened the sack which Cymon had thrown down, drawing out many treasures.

Along with the pearls, there was a silver plate and a large golden goblet, ornate, as though cast for some sort of prize. A jewellery box and several expensive looking books completed the haul, and Mr. Gobler nodded with satisfaction as Cymon bid them goodnight.

"Look at me, I am the Queen of England," Tomkins said, holding the pearls up to his neck and jumping up onto the table.

"Give me those, Tomkins. They will make a pretty penny in Cheapside at the pawnbrokers. You are to go there tomorrow, take Miss Olivia and Miss Mabel Marie with you. Perhaps this time they can be of some assistance. See what they can do," Mr. Gobler said, and he smiled at Olivia and Mabel Marie.

"We are to thieve?" Olivia asked, and Mr. Gobler laughed.

"Soon, it will become like second nature to you, my dears. But now, come, sit, we must all eat and hear about your adventures today," he said, ushering them to the table where a fine feast was once more laid out for them.

***

The next day, after another breakfast of bacon and eggs, Olivia and Mabel Marie found themselves in the company of Tomkins, Wisbottle, O'Bleary, and Beadle, making their way through the streets toward Cheapside, the haul of goods which Cymon Tuggs had brought them safely stowed about their persons.

"The pawnbroker is a good man, a man who asks few questions and pays handsomely. You let me do the talking, you hear?" Tomkins said, as they came to a narrow street where the houses hung almost together, and small shops and businesses lined the way.

The pawnbrokers had just opened, and the six children stepped inside the shop, which was filled with an astonishing array of goods and trinkets. A tall, wiry man stood behind the counter and he fixed them with a smile as they entered, evidently knowing what was to come.

"Well now, boys, what have you brought for me today, then?" he asked, as Tomkins opened his waistcoat, the jewellery from the stolen box hanging down from his lapels.

"A few items that Mr. Gobler thinks may interest you, Mr. Harvey," Tomkins said, and he held up each piece to the light, as the pawnbroker nodded and smiled.

"Oh yes, very fine. And I suppose Mr. Gobler chanced upon these quite by accident, did he?" he said, winking at them.

"Quite by accident, sir. Mr. Gobler has long been a man of charity and a good Christian soul. He was in the habit of visiting an elderly lady in Primrose Hill, a Duchess, no less. He brought her such comfort in her old age that when, last week, she should meet her death most peacefully, a fact which caused Mr. Gobler such heartache, sir, well, to his surprise, sir, she left him a sizable inheritance. As you can appreciate, sir, Mr. Gobler has no need for precious jewels and would far rather the money were in shillings and notes, so that he might use it for the charitable purposes to which he is so accustomed," O'Bleary said, and the man nodded.

"Oh, Mr. Gobler is a most charitable man, and how kind of the Duchess to make this gift to him," he said, holding up the string of pearls.

"He is distraught at her death, sir. A man with a soul such as Mr. Gobler feels such loss in his heart," Wisbottle said, and the pawnbroker raised his eyebrow.

"All right, Wisbottle, save me the sanctimony. I shall give you three guineas for the lot," the pawnbroker said, and Tomkins nodded.

"It is always a pleasure doing business with you, Mr. Harvey and I am sure that Mr. Gobler will soon have more items in his … inherit," he said, taking the money which the pawnbroker offered him, before the six of them stepped back out onto the street.

"I have never seen so much money," Olivia said, and Tomkins and the others laughed.

"Sometimes we thieve three times as much in a day," he replied.

"Once we stole ten guineas from a Duke," Beadle said, a proud smile coming over his face.

"And now it is your turn, Miss Olivia, Miss Mabel Marie. Mr. Gobler wants you to act as decoy, and I know just the place to do it," Tomkins said, and beckoning them to follow him, he ran off along the street.

Olivia and Mabel Marie had no choice but to follow, and the six children ran through Canning Town toward the river where the dirty back alleys soon gave way to wide and elegant streets, built in the Georgian style and where fashionable ladies and gentlemen promenaded to be seen.

"There, Tomkins, look," Beadle said, pointing to where a man and a woman stood at a flower stall, the gentleman having just bought his companion a dozen red roses.

"Just the ticket. Look, he has just put his pocketbook into his tailcoat pocket. You two ladies distract him, and I will do the thieving," Tomkins said, turning to Olivia and Mabel Marie.

"But what are we to do?" Olivia said, and Tomkins smiled.

"Tell the lady that your mother is very ill and that you must have a penny to buy bread for her, else she will starve to death. Yes, that will work nicely," he said, and before Olivia could respond, they pushed her and Mabel Marie forward, almost knocking into the woman who looked up in surprise.

"Away with you, urchins," the man said, but the woman tutted.

"Really, Charles, they are only little girls. What is it, dears?" she asked, and Olivia looked up at her, wide eyed, her heart beating faster than it had ever done before.

She had a kindly look about her powdered cheeks, and a sweet lavender scent. Olivia thought she looked beautiful, and the thought of lying to her seemed too awful to comprehend.

"Please, miss, but our mother is very sick. May we beg a penny from you to buy bread for her?" Mabel Marie asked, and the woman smiled.

"Your poor, dear things. Did you hear that, Charles? Their mother is very sick. Here you are, dear," the woman said, taking out a silk purse and bringing out a shilling.

"A shilling is too much, Floretta," her companion said, and the woman tutted.

"And you have just spent ten shillings on Roses for me, Charles, a quite extraordinary amount. It is my allowance, and I shall do with it as I please," she said, and she handed the two shillings to Olivia, just as Tomkins lifted the gentleman's pocketbook from his frock tails.

"Thank you, miss," Mabel Marie said, and Olivia smiled up at the woman.

"Yes, thank you, our mother will be ever so grateful to you. God bless you," she said, and the woman smiled a pretty smile.

"And God bless you, my dears. Good day to you, goodbye," she said, as Olivia and Mabel Marie ran off into the crowd.

"Like true professionals," Tomkins said, holding up the pocketbook, "I think the two of you will fit in very well."

Olivia glanced back through the crowd, watching as the man and woman disappeared from sight. It had felt so deceptive to trick her like that, a wrong which would surely one day find her out. But Olivia had no more time to think in such a way, for already Tomkins had selected their next victim and was busy instructing Olivia and Mabel Marie in what distraction to employ next …

Chapter 7
An Uncomfortable Plan

Olivia and Mabel Marie clattered through the door into the attic above the warehouse. It was pouring, and it soaked them through to the skin, glad of the warmth from the fire and a chance to shake off their wet petticoats and shawls. Mr. Gobler looked up and smiled at them. He was cooking sausages over the fire and laid down the frying pan, hurrying over to greet them, a greedy look in his eyes.

"Well now, my dears, what do my two favourite ladies have for me this afternoon?" he said, as Olivia rummaged in her pockets and drew out their day's takings.

"A pocket watch, six handkerchiefs of the finest silk, a pocketbook with twenty shillings in notes, and this fine, leather-bound notebook," Olivia said, and Mr. Gobler smiled and ran his tongue over his teeth.

"Yes, Miss Olivia, well done, and you too Miss Mabel Marie. Look at this, boys, you could all learn something from our dear young ladies," he said, beckoning Tomkins, Wisbottle, O'Bleary, and Beadle over from the table where they had sat playing cards.

"No one ever suspects the ladies," Tomkins said, smiling at Olivia, who nodded.

"Surely that is enough for today?" she said, for she was tired and the two of them had been out on the streets since early that morning.

"It is, of course it is, my dears. Come and sit yourselves down by the fire and make yourselves warm. A little something to eat, perhaps?" Mr. Gobler said, and Olivia and Mabel Marie nodded.

They were both twelve years old now and had lived in the attic above the warehouse with Mr. Gobler and his boys ever since their arrival in London all those years before. Mabel Marie was no nearer to finding her mother, though Artemis had made enquiries here and thereabouts, but one thing was certain and that was that the streets of London were not paved with gold as the two girls had believed.

The years since their arrival had been long, and they had found themselves under the subjection of Mr. Gobler who, though always the very model of kindliness, had made it clear where their loyalties should lie. With nowhere else to go, the two girls had remained in the company of Tomkins, Wisbottle, O'Bleary, Beadle, and all the rest, learning the art of thievery to the very highest standards.

"Where did you steal all that from? Kentish Town?" Beadle asked, as Mr. Gobler handed each of the girls a plate of sausages and fried potatoes.

"Primrose Hill, everyone knows that Primrose Hill is best for pick-pocketing," Olivia said, and Beadle laughed.

"Listen to her, Mr. Gobler, anyone would think she was the Queen of thieving," he said.

"Well she is, you could all learn a thing or two from Miss Olivia," Mr. Gobler replied, winking at Olivia.

"It is the hands. What did I say when first she arrived here?" a voice from the corner of the attic piped up.

Cymon Tuggs was sitting in an armchair, his boots kicked off and a pipe in his mouth, wreathed in tobacco smoke. Olivia had not noticed him when first she had returned, too intent upon getting dry and warm, but now she looked at him in surprise, holding out her hands, which appeared as nothing special.

"What do you mean, Mr. Tuggs?" she asked, and he rose to his feet.

"Hands, Miss Olivia, the delicate hands are the ones best for thieving. Hands that can slip in and out without being seen … or felt," he replied, stepping forward into the light of the fire.

"And we shall need those hands, Mr. Tuggs, shall we not?" Artemis said, grinning at Olivia, as Cymon nodded.

"That we will, Mr. Gobler, that we will," Cymon replied, and a ripple of laughter ran through the attic, as the other boys now crowded round.

Olivia glanced nervously at Mabel Marie, fearing that they were about to be embroiled in yet more immoral works, for despite their skills at the art of pick-pocketing it remained an undertaking which each found repulsive and wicked.

"Now, my dears, listen to Mr. Tuggs, for he has a special plan for you. A very special plan," Mr. Gobler said, rubbing his hands together.

"There is a gentleman named Sir Stanley Evenson, who owns a large house on Foxville Road, not a mile or so from here, a gentleman who has recently come into a great inheritance, though he was wealthy already. A large garden surrounded the house, with shrubbery in which to hide. I had been in the area recently and spied some very attractive looking pieces of silver and gold through the windows of the gentleman's study. He does not need more wealth and it will be an easy enough thing for us to take it from him," Cymon said.

"But what are we to do?" Olivia asked, and Cymon smiled.

"There is a window leading into the scullery which is never shut because Lady Evenson's cats use it to slip in and out of. The window is small, no bigger than a child's width, hence why it is never closed, no bigger than ... you, Olivia," Cymon said, looking her up and down with a nod of satisfaction.

"But she cannot do that," Mabel Marie said, looking anxiously at Olivia, who felt her hands shaking.

"Of course, she can, Miss Mabel Marie. If she can steal a pocket watch, then she can slip easily into a gentleman's study and pass the silver out of the window to Mr. Tuggs here," Mr. Gobler said, his tongue running over his teeth, as he brought the tips of his fingers together and smiled.

"I ... I do not know. We have done everything asked of us and ..." Olivia began, but Mr. Tuggs raised his hand.

"Then it is all settled then. Tomorrow night, at the stroke of midnight. Meet me beneath the clock tower of Saint Michael's, come with Tomkins, he can help to carry the loot," he said, and without waiting for a reply, he slipped out of the attic and was away into the night.

Olivia looked nervously around her and Mr. Gobler smiled. "Get some rest now, my dear. You shall stay here tomorrow, no thieving during the day, for this is far too important a task for you to spoil yourself," he said, and the others nodded.

"If you do this, Olivia, we shall know you as the greatest thief in all of London, the greatest lady thief that is," Wisbottle said.

"There have been lady thieves before, but none so talented as Miss Olivia, here," Mr. Gobler said, and he hummed to himself, turning back toward the fire to warm his hands.

Olivia felt sick to her stomach at the thought of what Mr. Tuggs had proposed, but what choice did she have but to follow his instructions? When she and Mabel Marie were alone that night, behind the curtain which separated their bunks from those of the boys, Olivia climbed up onto the top bunk and slipped into bed beside her closest friend.

"I do not think I can do it," she whispered, and Mabel Marie put her arms around her and hugged her.

"I wish we could both go. I do not envy you going alone. It is one thing to thieve upon the streets, but another to enter the house of a gentleman like that and steal his valuables. What if they catch you?" she whispered back.

"Then I will go before the magistrate, there will be no escaping," she said, and Mabel Marie sobbed.

"I cannot lose you, Olivia, please be careful," she begged.

Olivia could barely sleep that night, imagining all the terrible things which could so easily go wrong if they caught her breaking into the house. She barely ate a thing at breakfast, sitting by the fire, as Mr. Gobler spoke excitedly about the night to come.

"It will be easy, my dear. Mr. Tuggs tells me that the gentleman has been foolish enough to keep all his precious wares on display. A boastful man is not a man who will suffer loss easily. Simply make your way into the study, open the window which will be locked from the inside, and pass the treasures out to Mr. Tuggs, then follow him home. You will be safely in your bed by the time the clocks strike one o'clock, and all of us shall be rich," he said, patting her on the head.

"But what if I am caught?" she asked, and Mr. Gobler looked at her with a smile.

"That is always the risk for any in our noble profession. But have you ever been caught before?" he said, and Olivia shook her head.

"No," she said, for though she despised it, she was an excellent thief, unrivalled even by Tomkins himself.

"Then why will this time be any different, my dear? No, you will return to us a hero– a heroine– and tomorrow morning I shall take you to Piccadilly and you shall choose a fancy dress and I will wear my best tails and we shall take tea with the Duchesses in a fine coffee house. What say you to that, my dear?" he asked, and Olivia nodded.

She would do her best to please him, to please them all, but that did not take away her fears, or the ever-present sense that what they intended was wrong. She had grown to despise the life she had found here for herself, as preferable as it might be to that of the orphanage. Here, in the company of Mr. Gobler and his boys, she had discovered a talent, but it was one which bore little fruit for herself, only for the profit of others, a profit of ill-gotten gains.

"I will try," she replied, and Mr. Gobler smiled.

"There, my dear, what a good girl you have become," he said, and went off humming to himself.

Olivia tried to distract herself for the rest of the day, helping Mabel Marie with the cooking and playing cards with O'Bleary and Beadle. But nothing could take away her fears at the approaching midnight hour. When they had eaten dinner, though Olivia struggled even to finish half her plate, she and Tomkins readied themselves to meet Mr. Tuggs outside the church.

"Are you ready? Tomkins said, and Olivia nodded, turning to Mabel Marie, who put her arms around her and kissed her on both cheeks.

"Please be careful," she whispered.

"Come along, my dear. Do not keep Mr. Tuggs waiting," Mr. Gobler said, and he hurried them both out of the door and into the dark night.

The smell of rancid meat hit her nostrils, a smell which, despite Tomkins' assurances, Olivia had never gotten used to and she swallowed hard, her hands shaking, as she followed Tomkins down to the yard below. It was deserted now, a frigid chill in the air and the moon shining down upon them. Tomkins led her through the gate and out onto the street. A chestnut seller, with burning coals in an upturned barrel, was still plying his trade on a corner, but the street was largely deserted, candles burning in the upstairs windows of the houses and those whose business brought them out at night stalking the streets.

"This way, Olivia, stay close to me," Tomkins said, and the two of them hurried toward the church, the spire of which reached high into the starry sky above.

As the clock struck the midnight hour, Cymon appeared out of the shadows, startling Olivia, who turned to find him dressed in a long black cloak and his signature battered top hat. He was carrying an empty bag slung over his shoulder and he beckoned for them both to follow him.

"Quickly now, the sooner we go, the sooner we shall return," he hissed, and hurried off into the darkness, with Olivia and Tomkins following behind.

He led them from the church and up the street, taking a left and a right. They came into a large square, with a garden at its centre and grand houses lying all around. Another street led off from it and Cymon pointed to the sign, which Olivia presumed read 'Foxville Road' for she still could not read.

"Are we close?" Olivia asked, and Cymon nodded.

"Not far. We shall creep into the garden and see if the family is safely asleep," he said, beckoning them to follow him.

A few moments later, they came to a large house set back from the road and surrounded by railings. A gate led into the garden and Cymon crept through, hiding at once amidst the shrubbery, as Olivia and Tomkins followed behind. There were no lights burning in the windows of the house, the shutters closed, the family evidently in their beds.

"What a place," Tomkins said, rubbing his hands together gleefully.

"The study is there and see that little window? That is the scullery," Cymon said, pointing through the bushes.

Olivia peered through the darkness. The scullery window was open, just as Cymon had said, though it was indeed no bigger than Olivia herself, and no man could have fitted through it.

"And what am I to do when I am inside?" she asked.

"Find your way to the study and open the shutters, open the window, and I shall come to take the silver. Hand it all out to me and then climb out yourself. We shall be on our way then," Cymon said, and without warning, he pushed Olivia forward.

She hurried across the garden, gazing up at the house as she did, fearful that at any moment they would see her. But the house was silent, and she came to the scullery window without incident, climbing up onto the ledge and hauling herself through. Once she was inside, she looked back across the garden to where she could just see Cymon and Tomkins hiding in the bushes. They made no movement, and she turned to look around her.

They filled the larder with many good things to eat, a large pie standing on a stand to her right and a dozen loaves of bread lined up on a shelf, with jars of pickles and preserves all around. Just then, a sudden movement caught her eye and she let out a cry, as a shadow flitted in the darkness, jumping up and flashing past her. She breathed a great sigh of relief, realising it was only one cat, which now slunk out into the night, leaving her to catch her breath.

"Come on Olivia, you can do this," she whispered to herself, and steadying her nerves, she crept out of the larder and into the dark kitchen beyond.

Chapter 8
A Clatter in the Night!

As Olivia's eyes adjusted to the darkness, she could make out a large kitchen table and a range running along one side of the kitchen, and an open door at the far side with a short flight of steps leading up to a hallway beyond. There was a lingering smell of cooking in the air, roasted meat, or fowl, and Olivia tried her best to think of being back in the attic with Mr. Gobler and the others.

She edged her way forward, listening intently for any sounds from above. But the house was quiet, and she stepped out into the hallway, trying to get her bearings, and wondering which door led to the study. In front of her lay the front door, barred and bolted, and to her right and left two doors, each leading into what she presumed were drawing rooms.

A large aspidistra plant lay on a table in the centre of the hallway and a staircase ran up to a landing above. Behind her, two further doors opened, one of which was ajar. She crept toward it, pushing it open and freezing as it creaked. But the door opened into the very room she sought, an enormous desk and shelves lined with books showing that this was Sir Stanley Evenson's study.

The window was shuttered, the only light coming from the moonlight which streamed into the hallway from glass panels either side of the front door. She felt about for the shutter catch, lifting it, and pulling them back to reveal the garden beyond. When he saw her, Cymon emerged from the shrubbery and ran toward the window, closely followed by Tomkins behind. The latch was easy to unclasp and Olivia slid the window up as Cymon leaned through.

"Well done, Olivia, now, hand me the silver from that shelf there," he said, pointing through the window to where the moonlight now illuminated a dozen silver plates displayed on a shelf above the fireplace.

Olivia went to pick up the first one. It was heavy, her hands shaking as she held it. She passed it through the window and Cymon snatched it greedily, stuffing it into the bag and pointing to the next one.

"Quickly, Olivia," Tomkins hissed.

Olivia hurried back to the shelf, picking up two plates and returning to the window, eager to finish the task as quickly as possible.

"And the rest. Come along, Olivia," Cymon hissed.

Olivia tried to pick up three of the plates at once, but her hands were shaking so much that one now fell to the floor with a great clatter, the sound of which echoed through the still and silent night. She froze as the sound of voices came from up above. In a flash, Cymon and Tomkins were gone, and Olivia ran for the window.

But as Tomkins had darted away, the frame had come clattering down with a bang, the latch jamming, as Olivia tried desperately to open it. But she could not hold it open and climb through, the frame too heavy for her shaking hands, and a moment later, the door to the study flew open and two figures appeared, footmen, rushing toward her and seizing hold of her.

"You just wait there, my lad," one of them said, as they dragged her out into the hallway where a candle was held up to her face, half a dozen others now crowded around her.

"Good heavens, but this is no thief, only a child, a girl," a woman exclaimed, and they all looked at her in astonishment.

***

Olivia was too terrified to speak. She struggled feebly in the arms of the footman, as much commotion ensued around her.

"Please, let me go. I have done nothing wrong," she said, as candles were lit, and several of the men entered the study.

"The silver plates, three of them are gone," came a cry from inside.

"So, you have done nothing wrong?" one footman said, still clutching Olivia tightly in his arms, as the man returned from the study.

He was older than the rest, with a kindly face, though one which now wore a frown. This was presumably Sir Stanley Evenson, and he peered at Olivia over his spectacles, a silk smoking jacket wrapped around him and a nightcap upon his head.

"You were not alone, that much I presume?" he said, and Olivia shook her head.

"Please, sir. I did not wish to do it. Really, I did not," she whispered, and he nodded.

"Bring her something to eat and a blanket to wrap around her shoulders. She is shivering. Bring her into the drawing room and have a fire kindled. I do not think any of us will sleep again tonight. Run for the constables, Andrew. There may still be some chance of catching the thieves," he said, pointing to one footman.

"But Sir Stanley, we have the thief," he replied, and the gentleman frowned.

"We have a scared little girl, that is what we have, and we shall take care of her until the proper authorities arrive," he said, and the footman nodded.

They led Olivia into a room at the front of the house and a fire was hastily lit. Sir Stanley took a seat opposite her, next to a woman who he introduced as his wife Lillian, a pretty woman with long golden hair and bright green eyes. The housekeeper was a Mrs. Mason, and she brought Olivia a piece of the meat pie she had seen in the larder, along with a slice of fruit cake and a glass of milk.

"Thank you, sir," Olivia said, glancing nervously at Sir Stanley and wondering what would now become of her.

"You were trying to steal the silver plates? How did you get in?" Sir Stanley said when Olivia had finished eating.

"Please, sir. Through the larder window," Olivia said, and Sir Stanley turned to his wife.

"You and your cats, my dear," he said, shaking his head.

"And then I was to open the study window and pass the plates out to ... to pass the plates out," Olivia said, not willing to reveal the identity of Cymon and Tomkins to the gentleman, as kind as he had been to her.

"They forced you to do this?" Sir Stanley asked, and Olivia nodded.

"The noble art of the pickpocket, though I suppose this is more than picking your pocket," she replied, and Sir Stanley laughed.

"It is hardly a noble art, Miss ...?" he said.

"Olivia, sir," she replied.

"Olivia, what?" he asked.

"Just Olivia, sir. I have no other name," she said, as Sir Stanley looked gravely at his wife.

"You poor thing," she said, "oh, Stanley, what can we do to help her? She has clearly lived a miserable life."

"May I leave, I am sorry, and I promise I will not thieve here again," Olivia said, desperate to escape and return to the attic above the warehouse.

She knew that Mabel Marie would be dreadfully worried about her, Mr. Gobler too, for Cymon and Tomkins would surely have returned with the sad news by now.

"It is not that simple, Olivia. I cannot just let you go, not after what has happened," Sir Stanley said, as a commotion in the hallway announced the metropolitan constabulary.

"Sir Stanley, I understand there has been a disturbance here. Let me assure you we shall do all we can to recover your stolen property and see justice done against these wicked men," a man in an Inspector's uniform and cape said, as he stepped into the room.

"Not just men, Inspector, and not all of them wicked," Sir Stanley said, pointing at Olivia, who now felt even more frightened than before.

"A girl? Well, sir, a girl can be a thief just as well as a boy. I have discovered that well enough in my time, I assure you. Come along, young lady, we shall deal with you. Did you catch her, red handed, so to speak, sir?" the Inspector asked.

"I did, Inspector, but I wish no punishment enacted upon her. She is a victim in all of this, forced into the work they made her to do," Sir Stanley said, and the Inspector looked at him in surprise.

"But if she is the accessory to a crime, then she should be punished, sir," the Inspector said, furrowing his brow in confusion.

"No, Inspector, I want you to find the men responsible for this and see that you return my three silver plates. The girl should not be punished," he said, and the Inspector nodded.

"Very well, Sir Stanley, you are a man of high standing and I shall do as you say, though it seems odd to me," he replied, shaking his head, "An orphanage perhaps, then? Rather than the juvenile prison."

"Oh, Stanley, no, we cannot have the poor child sent away to an orphanage," Lillian cried, as Olivia's heart skipped a beat.

Would they take her back to Craddock's and the cruel clutches of Mr. and Mrs. Dounce? Even after all these years they would surely be angry with her, cruel to her, and punish her. Tears welled up in her eyes and she looked imploringly at Sir Stanley, who shook his head.

"I have visited such places, they are inhumane, I will not see the girl sent there. No ... very well, she will remain here," he said, and the Inspector raised his eyebrows.

"She is a street urchin, Sir Stanley, and she will only bring you trouble. There will be a gang of them, believe me, I know, you will have no peace," he said, scowling at Olivia, who cowered under his gaze.

"Inspector, I shall be the judge of that if you will permit me. I hardly see a criminal mastermind before me, but a scared and innocent little girl who needs a warm bed and someone to take care of her. My wife and I have but one child, and we have always dearly wished for another. Permit me to offer this charity, for it is surely written that he who shows charity to the stranger shows it to Christ himself," Sir Stanley said, an argument for which the Inspector clearly had no ready response.

"Very well, sir, if you will excuse me it appears I have two criminals to catch," and he eyed Olivia with suspicion.

"And I am sure you will do an admirable job in doing so," Sir Stanley replied.

"But she must know something, sir. A girl does not simply become an accomplice. Come on, tell me what you know," he said, rounding on Olivia, who shrunk back in fear.

"Inspector, she is only a child, and terrified," Lillian said, and she put her arm protectively around Olivia and drew her into her skirts.

"Well, if she remembers anything, then perhaps you would be so good as to inform me, Lady Evenson?" he said, clearly growing exasperated.

"We shall, but for now we must wish you a goodnight," Sir Stanley said, and they escorted the Inspector out into the hallway.

When the door had closed, Sir Stanley turned to Olivia and smiled, shaking his head and gazing down at her affectionately.

"We must put her to bed, Stanley, and in the morning, we can decide what to do," his wife said, and Sir Stanley nodded.

"Yes. Andrew, see that we secure the window and have the larder window shut and bolted. The cats will just have to ask if they wish to go out," he stated, smiling at his wife, who laughed.

"Mrs. Mason, would you take Olivia upstairs and settle her, sit with her until she is asleep," Lillian said, and the housekeeper placed a gentle hand upon Olivia's shoulder.

"This way, my dear," she said, and she led Olivia up the carpeted staircase to a landing above, with doors opening on every side along a corridor.

Candles burned there, illuminating portraits and paintings along the walls. Fine pieces of furniture lined the corridor, and another flight of stairs led to the next floor above. A large arched window allowed moonlight to flood in at one end, the stars twinkling in the sky, and Mrs. Mason led Olivia to the far end, unlocking a door and ushering her inside.

They prettily furnished the room with an enormous bed covered by a canopy and made up with deep blankets and rugs. There was a fireplace with a freshly laid fire, to which Mrs. Mason now struck a match, the room soon flickering with the warmth of the flames. Further pieces of furniture lined the walls and a thick curtain hung at the window, so that Olivia could hardly believe her eyes at the comfort and delight of it all.

"Am I to sleep here?" she asked, looking up at Mrs. Mason with wide eyes.

"You are, and in the morning, you shall have some porridge, bacon, eggs, whatever you desire," she said, and Olivia smiled.

"Mr. Gobler always makes us bacon and eggs, he says that it 'sets us up for the day,' and we always have seconds," she replied, forgetting herself for a moment.

"Mr. Gobler?" the housekeeper replied, and Olivia bit her tongue.

"I mean … I did not," she began, fearing the betrayal, but Mrs Mason only pulled back the blankets on the bed and lifted her in.

"There now, you must try to rest. I will sit by the fire until you go off and then come for you in the morning. You are quite safe here, Sir Stanley and his wife are the most delightful of people and in the morning, you shall meet Arthur, too," she said, as Olivia yawned.

"Arthur?" she asked, suddenly feeling ever so sleepy.

"Sir Stanley's son, he is about your age and a delightful boy," she said, and leaning down, the housekeeper kissed Olivia on her forehead, before tucking her into bed.

"Am I to stay here?" Olivia asked, and Mrs. Mason smiled.

"Only if you want to, but you would be a fool not to. Come now, off to sleep with you, my dear," she said, taking up the candle she had set by the bedside and snuffing it out, before taking a chair by the fire to wait for Olivia to fall asleep.

The fire crackled in the hearth and Olivia felt safe and warm tucked up in the cosy room. It was quite a contrast to her bunk in the attic at the warehouse, with its stench of the abattoir, and a dozen boys sleeping cheek by jowl. She wondered what had become of Cymon and Tomkins. Had they gotten away? And what of Mabel Marie? She would be terribly worried when she discovered they had caught Olivia. But now, sleep came over her and her thoughts turned to dreams, her fortunes having taken a surprising turn for the better.

Chapter 9
An Unexpected Turn

Olivia awoke with a start. For a moment, she did not know where she was and she sat up, rubbing her eyes, and looking around her. The curtains had been pulled back slightly, allowing a shaft of light to enter the room, the signs of a dull grey day visible through the window. The fire had burned to nothing, a few glowing embers remaining, and Olivia turned to get out of bed, the events of the night gradually returning.

But to her great surprise, she realised she was not alone, and she let out a gasp, shrinking back into the blankets, as a boy, no older than herself, stepped out of the shadows. He was smartly dressed, a gentleman in miniature, with blue tails and a pressed shirt with a cravat at the neck. He wore black breeches and highly polished shoes and he looked at her curiously, a smile playing across his face.

"You were naughty," he said, and Olivia blushed.

"I did not mean to," she replied, and he laughed.

"It must have been quite an adventure climbing through my father's study window like that. I wish I could be a thief, I would be the best thief in all of London and never get caught," he said, taking another step forward and looking her up and down.

"It was not my choice," she said, and he looked at her in surprise.

"Then whose choice was it?" he asked, evidently having heard the full story from his father and mother.

Olivia remained silent. She had already made the mistake of mentioning Mr. Gobler and she was not about to reveal any more, however kind the family were.

"Oh, Master Arthur, I see you have already met our guest," Mrs. Mason said, as she bustled into the room, much to Olivia's relief.

"She was telling me about her adventures," Arthur replied, and Mrs. Mason laughed.

"I think we have had enough of adventures for one night. Come along, my dear, you shall come downstairs and take your breakfast in the dining room. We must find you some new clothes today as well, you can hardly sit with the Master in those old rags you were wearing. Now, Master Arthur, give Miss Olivia some privacy whilst I get her washed, you can speak to her later on," Mrs. Mason said, and Arthur nodded.

"Bye," he said, and Olivia smiled.

"Bye," she replied, deciding that she rather liked him, though she must still be wary of what she said.

"Master Arthur slept all the way through the excitement last night. It terribly disappointed him when he woke up this morning and learned all about it," the housekeeper said, as she helped Olivia to dress.

"Please, Mrs. Mason, what will happen to me?" Olivia asked, as the housekeeper scrubbed her face with warm soapy water.

She looked down at Olivia and smiled.

"Sir Stanley and his wife are good people. If you want to stay here, then you shall. But I am sure they will find some jobs for you to do. Master Arthur is away at school and I could always do with help around the house. Can you sew and cook?" she asked, and Olivia nodded.

"Mabel Marie is the better cook, but I have learned to sew, and I am good at pick-pocketing," she said, once again forgetting herself.

Mrs. Mason raised her eyebrows and then laughed, shaking her head as she dried Olivia's face.

"Well, there will be no need for any of that anymore, that is for certain. Come along, my dear, let me take you downstairs for something to eat. The Master is waiting for you," she said, and giving Olivia a last glance up and down, she took her by the hand and led her downstairs.

As they came down to the hallway, the smell of breakfast cooking wafted through the air and two large Persian cats rolled in on the rug in a ray of weak sunshine coming through the hallway window. They looked up as Olivia approached, coming to slink and purr around her legs, as Olivia leant down to stroke them.

"Archibald and Marmaduke," Lillian said, as she emerged from the dining room, smiling at Olivia who now sat down on the hallway floor and allowed the cats to clamber onto her.

"Now, Miss Olivia, show a little decorum," Mrs. Mason said, but Lillian only laughed.

"Do you like cats, Olivia?" she asked, and Olivia nodded, as Archibald rubbed his head into her chin and let out a loud meow.

"They are very beautiful," Olivia said.

"Come and have your breakfast, then you may play with them in the morning room, they enjoy sitting there when the sun is coming through the windows, cats love the sunlight," Lillian said, offering Olivia her hand and leading her into the dining room.

Sir Stanley was tucking vigorously into a plate of devilled kidneys and he looked up at Olivia and smiled, beckoning her to take a seat at his side, as one maid brought in fresh coffee and toast.

"Did you sleep well, Olivia?" he asked, and she nodded.

"Oh, yes, thank you, sir, it was a most comfortable bed," she replied, gazing in awe at the beautifully laid table with its gleaming silver cutlery and gold rimmed crockery.

"I suppose you are not used to such comforts. Please, help yourself to breakfast, there is kedgeree in the tureen there, bacon and eggs, sausages and black pudding, porridge too, with honey and sugar, whatever you desire," he said, pointing to the sideboard which groaned under the weight of food.

Olivia looked at it wide eyed. She was used to Mr. Gobler's cooking, but this was something else. Did Sir Stanley eat like this every day? With shaking hands, she took a plate and helped herself from the sideboard, just as the door burst open and Arthur came bounding in, filled with excitement.

"Father, the wind has picked up, we can fly the kite today. Oh, do say we can," he said, holding a large paper kite in hand, decorated with a long-ribboned tail and painted red and gold.

Sir Stanley laughed, nodding to Arthur, who took up a plate and joined Olivia at the sideboard.

"You have already had your breakfast, Master Arthur, you cannot be hungry again," Mrs. Mason said, as she entered the room with a dish of eggs in hand.

"That was nearly an hour ago, Mrs. Mason, *of course* I am hungry again," Arthur said, grinning at Olivia, as he piled his plate high with sausages and bacon.

"You shall need a substantial breakfast if we are to fly the kite this morning. We will go up onto the common, it will be even windier there," Sir Stanley replied.

He had omitted the incident the night before and it was almost as though the matter were entirely settled and Olivia had simply become part of the family overnight. She returned to the table, taking up her knife and fork and eating, as Arthur sat next to her and continued to talk enthusiastically about his kite.

"I am an excellent flyer, I built this kite myself, with a little help from my father," he said, tucking into his second breakfast with gusto.

"Perhaps Olivia would like to come and see you fly it," Sir Stanley said, "have you flown a kite before, Olivia?" and Olivia shook her head.

"No, sir," she replied, and he smiled.

"Then you shall fly one this morning. Come along, children, the sooner you eat up the sooner we shall be out in the fresh air," he said, rubbing his hands together with glee.

Olivia could not help but like Sir Stanley and his wife, they had such a kind way about them, and nothing seemed too much trouble. They were the complete opposite to Mr. and

Mrs. Dounce, and Olivia had taken to them immediately, though her thoughts were still on the events of the previous night and of its consequences.

"Please, Sir Stanley, what is to become of me?" she asked, just as Lillian entered the dining room.

Sir Stanley looked at his wife and the two of them smiled.

"Well, Olivia, you have lived a hard life, we really know nothing about you, but it would be remiss of me to send you away, and I would not have you sent to the workhouse or an orphanage. Those places are scourges upon our society, and the thought of you in such a place is just too much to bear. You must understand that you have been a victim in all of this, for I highly doubt that it was your idea to break into this house last night," Sir Stanley said, and Olivia shook her head.

"No, sir, it was because of my hands," she said, holding them out to Sir Stanley, who looked at her in surprise.

"Your hands?" he asked, a puzzled note in his voice.

"Yes sir, Mr. Go … they say I have small hands, just right for pick-pocketing and getting through small spaces," she said, embarrassed by what she was admitting.

"You need never use your hands in such a way again, if you would like to stay here then you are very welcome to do so. Mrs. Mason could use some help around the house. But I do not think of those who work for me as servants. We are all one family here," he said, and Olivia smiled.

It turned out that Sir Stanley was a man of great learning, who had written several influential books on the proper systems of government and the rights of man. He had ideas which many believed modern and out of place, but which in practice brought significant benefit to those over whom he had influence, not least his household, all of whom appeared happy in his employ.

When breakfast was concluded and they had found new clothes for Olivia–having formerly belonged to Mrs. Mason's own daughter–so that she looked quite the part next to Arthur, they set out for the common. The wind had picked up now, so that Arthur declared it the perfect conditions to fly his kite, and Sir Stanley enthused how high they might see the kite soar into the sky.

"Do you really mean to say you have never flown a kite before?" he asked, as they came to the top of the common, and Olivia shook her head.

"I never have, no, we did not play when I was younger," she said, remembering the sad days spent at Craddock's Correction House, when the most amusement they derived was from simple games played at night in the dormitories or the occasional outing and a picnic.

"Not everyone has had the same opportunities as you, Arthur," his father replied, as they stood looking out over the common and the city spread out like a toy town below.

There were several others flying kites that morning, the wind lifting them soaring into the air, where they plunged and dived, ducked and rose, as shrieks of delight echoed all around.

"I will show you then," Arthur said, handing the kite string to his father, and unwinding it, as he ran backwards, ready to toss the kite into the air.

"You see, Olivia, he will wait for a strong gust and then throw it up, the wind will catch it and you shall see it rise into the sky," Sir Stanley said, and Olivia watched in fascination, as Arthur waited patiently for just the right moment.

Suddenly, a gust of wind shook the trees above and several others threw their kites into the air, just as Arthur let go of his. The gust took it, sending it straight up into the air, as Arthur let out a cry of delight. The string unfurled and Olivia watched as the kite soared into the sky above, rising so high that it seemed almost to touch the clouds.

"Look at that, Olivia, how wonderful," Sir Stanley said, as Arthur ran up and his father handed him the handle from which the string rose, pulling taut and tight.

"Olivia, you have a go," Arthur said, smiling at her as he handed her the handle.

They did not prepare her for the tug, and she almost fell forward with the force of the kite blowing up above.

"Steady there, hold her hand, Arthur," Sir Stanley said, and Arthur stood behind Olivia, his arms over her shoulder, helping to guide the kite.

"It is wonderful," Olivia exclaimed, for she had never felt so free before, allowed simply to be a child at play and without the cares and worries which so often beset her.

"Watch this, I will make it go in a circle," Arthur said, taking the kite handle from Olivia and pulling at the string, so that the kite dived and back up in a wide arc.

It was a marvellous sight, and the three spent a happy few hours on the common, flying the kite and watching others do the same. They returned home rosy cheeked and eager for refreshment, which was provided as an excellent luncheon of ham and parsley sauce with roasted potatoes and vegetables. Olivia and Arthur sat next to one another at the table and Archibald and Marmaduke lay at their feet, purring and letting out the occasional loud meow.

"Olivia was a natural with the kite," Sir Stanley said, as his wife asked the children to tell her about their morning on the common.

"It flew so high, Mother, I almost lost sight of it. Perhaps it even went to the moon," Arthur enthused, and his mother laughed.

"I think you would need a long piece of string for that, Arthur. Did you enjoy yourself, Olivia?" she asked, and Olivia nodded.

"Oh yes, thank you," Olivia said, smiling at Lillian, as she helped herself to more potatoes.

"And perhaps this afternoon you would like to read? I am sure Arthur would let you choose from his books," Lillian said, and Olivia blushed.

"I … I do not know how," she admitted, suddenly feeling terribly embarrassed.

She had never had cause to read, nor to learn, and besides, there was no one able to teach her, for Mr. Gobler could not read and neither could any of the others. But she had always liked the idea of doing so, for she knew books contained gateways into other worlds, places of escape and fantasy and stories of high adventure and excitement. Sir Stanley looked at her sympathetically and smiled.

"Perhaps Arthur will read to you and we shall plan for you to learn. It is very important that a child should learn to read. It will open up an undiscovered country," he said, and Olivia smiled.

"I would like to learn, for I have never had the opportunity," she said, and Lillian smiled.

"Then you shall learn, and much more besides that. For now, Arthur will read to you," she said, and Arthur nodded.

"I have lots of books to choose from, come along, I shall show you my playroom," he said, glancing at his mother, who nodded.

"Arthur thinks himself far too grown up for a nursery now. You may be excused," she said, and both children got down from the table.

The cats slinked after them and Arthur clattered up the stairs, beckoning Olivia to follow him.

"What kind of book would you like me to read to you? I have many adventure stories on my shelves," he said, leading her along the corridor toward the room she had spent the night in and pushing open a door to the right.

It was a most wonderful room, and Olivia gasped in delight. They filled it with toys, a large rocking horse sitting in the bay window and the walls covered in shelves of books. A large rug was spread out in the centre and it too was covered with yet more toys and games. They set a chess board to one side, and next to it a large model ship, complete with canon and sail. Olivia could hardly take it all in, as Arthur pointed to the shelves.

"I have never seen so many toys," she gasped, for she had never even owned a doll of her own, let alone seen a room such as this.

It was like a toy shop, resplendent with every delight the imagination of a child could conjure.

"Then you shall share them. My father says that if we all shared what we have a little more, then the world would be a far better place," Arthur said, and Olivia smiled, thinking back to Mr. Gobler's similar sentiments, though clearly, they were meant rather differently.

"What book will you read to me?" she asked, gazing at the spines, the words upon which meant nothing to her.

"This is my favourite," he said, pulling out a book with a picture of an island, covered in palm trees, on the front.

"What is it called?" she asked, and he opened it.

"*Robinson Crusoe,* it is all about an adventurer who is stranded upon a deserted island and who has to overcome terrible odds to return home," he said, settling himself down upon a chair by the fire.

"It sounds very exciting," she said, seating herself opposite and pulling her knees up to her chin.

"I was born in the Year 1632, in the City of York, of a good Family, tho' not of that Country, my Father being a Foreigner of Bremen, who settled first at Hull ..." Arthur began, and Olivia entered a world the likes of which she had never known before.

Chapter 10
A Past Reminder

Olivia soon settled into life with Sir Stanley and his family. He was the model of kindness and treated her with all the love and care which one would expect of a father. His wife too treated Olivia like the daughter she had never had, and Arthur delighted in having a sister to share his play with, the two soon becoming firm friends. He read her the whole of *Robinson Crusoe* in the days which followed and then began a book called *Treasure Island,* an adventure which enthralled Olivia and made her dream of far-off lands and strange, exotic peoples.

Hearing such stories made her think again of her own origins, for she knew nothing of where she had come from, nor whom her parents might be. She imagined mystery, though she knew the story would be banal and had resigned herself to the thought that neither her mother nor her father would ever be found, and if they were, their own story was likely to be as tragic as hers. But despite this, she was thankful for the turn in her own fortunes, grateful to Sir Stanley for all he had done for her.

When she was not playing with Arthur or learning her lessons from Lillian, Olivia would help Mrs. Mason around the house. She enjoyed watching her cook and had already learned a great deal from her. There were many jobs to do about the house and they set Olivia to work sewing, dusting, and fetching and carrying tasks which she was all too happy to assist with, given the generosity of her hosts. This was the family she had never had, and whilst she missed Mabel Marie terribly, she knew they had given her another chance. But still a terrible secret hung over her, and Olivia had not yet spoken of her years with Mr. Gobler and the others, still wary of revealing the truth, lest it led to terrible consequences for them all.

"Will you sweep the terrace for me, Olivia, my dear? Then you and Master Arthur will have your luncheon and can play," Mrs. Mason said, as Olivia entered the kitchen one morning.

She had been living with Sir Stanley and his family for two weeks now, and the ways of the household seemed second nature to her.

"Yes, of course," she said, taking up a stiff brush and pan from the corner, "Arthur is reading me *Treasure Island*, I wish I could go to a place like that."

"I am sure you have had your own adventures, Miss Olivia. As for me, I am happy in my kitchen. There are no cakes on a desert island," she said, and winked at Olivia with a smile.

It was a chilly day outside and they wrapped Olivia up against the cold. The terrace lay looking out over the gardens and was covered in leaves, the remnants of the winter fall. But the garden itself was bursting into life, filled with many beautiful plants and flowers. Lillian took great pride in the garden and she had explained to Olivia how she had planted fruit trees and trailing roses, the blossom of which was just bursting forth in brilliant pinks and whites.

Olivia swept, humming to herself as she went, a tune to a song which Arthur had taught her about a grand old Duke and his men who marched to the top of a hill. She was so taken up with her work that she did not notice the four figures hurrying across the lawn and who now came to the terrace steps, just as Olivia turned and let out a cry of surprise. Tomkins, Wisbottle, O'Bleary, and Beadle all stood grinning at her and she dropped her broom with a clatter as they advanced toward her.

"What are you doing here?" she hissed, anxious that no one should see them.

"Rescuing you, of course," Tomkins said, and the others nodded.

"We tried to come sooner, but we kept getting chased away. We have been hiding in the bushes all morning," Wisbottle said.

"Come on, there is a gap in the railings back there, we can all fit through it. Mr. Gobler has been so worried and Mabel Marie cannot stop crying," Beadle said, as Tomkins took Olivia by the arm.

"But I …" Olivia began, glancing back at the house where lamps burned in the windows and the smell of baking wafted from the kitchen.

She had become used to the happiness of life with Sir Stanley and his family and had no desire to leave. But she knew how much she owed to Mr. Gobler and the others, to Mabel Marie especially. Could she tear herself away from her old life and remain in this? Or was she destined to be a street urchin, an outcast from the society which the house and its household represented?

"Come on," Tomkins hissed, "we have little time, they shall see us."

But his words came too late, for the door to the kitchen had just opened and Arthur appeared with a bat and ball, staring at the scene before him in surprise.

"Olivia, what is all this?" he said, dropping the bat and ball and advancing towards them, "are these urchins causing you trouble? How dare you enter my father's garden like this, I shall summon the constable immediately."

"Arthur, no, it is all right, they are … known to me," Olivia replied.

"Too right we are known to you," Wisbottle said, as the four boys turned to face Arthur defiantly.

"Away with you, or I shall call the footmen to chase you. Be gone," Arthur cried, rolling up his sleeves, as though he would willingly fight the four of them single handed.

"Oh, please, no violence," Olivia cried, stepping between Arthur and the others, as they squared up to one another.

"But who are they? How do you know them?" Arthur asked, as tears welled up in Olivia's eyes and she looked desperately at Tomkins, her look imploring him to leave, as much as it pained her to do so.

It was as though she were upon a bridge, straddling two different worlds, her old life and her new. How confused she felt, how torn, and yet she knew there was but one right choice to make.

"We took care of her when no one else would, when the likes of you would have dismissed her for an urchin, just as you look down upon us now," Wisbottle growled, and the other three nodded.

"She should come with us where she belongs. This fancy house and you fancy types are not for the likes of an orphan like her," Tomkins said, and he stepped forward, as though about to make a grab at Olivia, who shrank back.

"How dare you," Arthur cried, and he shot forward, delivering a sharp blow to Tomkins, who fell back with a bloodied nose.

Arthur was an excellent boxer, having been instructed whilst away at school, and Tomkins was reeling from the pain, as the other three looked on in amazement.

"Come on, we are not wanted here," Tomkins said, shooting Olivia an angry glance, as the four boys ran off across the gardens and into the shrubbery.

"Olivia, are you all right? They did not hurt you?" Arthur said, turning to Olivia and putting his arm around her.

"No, they would not have done. But … oh, Arthur, I am sorry, I have not been truthful. Not with you, nor your father, and you have done so much to make me welcome here. I hardly deserve it," she said, as he led her back inside.

The kitchen was empty, Mrs. Mason gone off to see to her chores, and a large fruit cake stood on the table, just waiting to be sliced.

"Sit down, we shall have some cake and you shall steady your nerves," Arthur said, pointing to Mrs. Mason's chair by the fire.

He cut two slices of the fruit cake, handing Olivia the larger slice, before pulling up a chair opposite her and smiling.

"I wish you had not been involved; I am sorry. I would have bid them leave, truly I would have done," Olivia said, taking a large bite of cake.

"But who were they? How did you know such rough little urchins?" he asked, and Olivia took a deep breath.

"Because that is exactly what I am too," she replied, and she told him the truth as to everything which had occurred to her since the day she left the orphanage.

She explained how she and Mabel Marie had escaped and come by chance into the company of Mr. Gobler and his band of pickpockets. There could be no sense of honour in the 'art of the pickpocket' anymore. They were pickpockets, plain and simple. She told him of her exploits in the city and of how she had become adept at lifting tailcoats and slipping her hands into pockets. There was shame in what she told him, a sense of guilt running through her, but also a purging, as though in telling Arthur the truth she could begin again.

When her explanation had finished and he knew the litany of colourful characters and the events which had led to her arrival at the home of Sir Stanley and his family, Arthur let out a low whistle and shook his head. Olivia expected her dismissal to be short and swift, and she wondered whether even now she might return to the attic above the warehouse and to the only life she really knew. But Arthur laughed, taking a bite of cake and looking at her with wide eyes.

"What an adventurous life you have had," he exclaimed, and Olivia looked at him in surprise.

"I ... you are not angry with me?" she asked, and once again he laughed.

"Angry? Why would I be angry with you? You have done nothing wrong, you are the victim of sad circumstances. But under what circumstances. Tell me, what was it like to be in such danger and to take such risks?" he asked, and she blushed.

"I did not think of it. I did not like it, but what choice did I have? Mabel Marie and I had nowhere else to go. We owed Mr. Gobler a debt, one which was difficult to pay," she replied, once more feeling guilty at the thought of leaving her best friend behind.

"And Mabel Marie? She is still there? Those boys seemed mean and cruel," Arthur replied, but Olivia shook her head.

"Not at all, they are kind. Good, even. I am only sorry that you saw them in an unpleasant light. They wanted only to bring me home … I mean, back," she said, uncertain now where her home truly lay.

"And what do you want?" he asked.

For a moment, Olivia was uncertain. She looked around at the cosy kitchen, the smell of baking lingering in the air, the fire crackling in the hearth. She thought of her warm bed and of the lessons which Lillian was giving her, of the games which she and Arthur had played and the stories he had read to her. Could it be more than a temporary dream? Could this now be her life, or would she forever be the urchin she believed herself to be?

"I want to stay, but how can I? I have lied to you and to your father and mother," she said, as tears welled up in her eyes.

"You did what you thought was right, I would have done the same," Arthur said, and he reached out and placed his hand gently on hers, smiling at her.

"You are very kind, I do not deserve it," Olivia whispered, but Arthur only laughed.

"You have had a true adventure your whole life long, one that I can only dream of. But there is still something you have not told me, for your story begins at the orphanage. What about before that? Who were your parents, where did you come from?" he asked, and Olivia shook her head.

"That is something I do not know. My first memories are of the orphanage and before that I know of nothing. It is all a mystery to me, though one I would dearly love to solve. Mabel Marie came to London in search of her mother, too, though we discovered nothing of her either. I do not believe I will ever know where my true family is," Olivia replied, shaking her head sadly.

"Then all the more reason to remain here with the family you have now," Arthur declared, and that was precisely what Olivia did.

Chapter 11
A Family to Call Her Own

In the years which followed, Olivia grew into an intelligent, pretty, and good-hearted young lady, a credit to Sir Stanley and his wife, who loved her as though she were their own. Her days were spent helping Mrs. Mason with the domestic tasks and taking lessons from Lillian, who taught her to read and write, instructed her in French, and gave her lessons in the scriptures and on the pianoforte. It was a happy life and one which Olivia rejoiced in, for at last she found herself with the family she had always longed for.

They sent Arthur away to school, but he would return in the holidays, a time which Olivia looked forward to immensely. Then, the two of them would play together, and as they grew older, they grew closer, taking walks together in the parks or visiting the fashionable shops and coffeehouses of the city. Olivia's favourite pastime was the theatre and Sir Stanley had introduced her to the works of Shakespeare, along with the delights of the great composers and their works.

She was now eighteen years old and had lived with Sir Stanley and his family for six years. In that time, she had heard nothing more of Mr. Gobler and the pickpockets, nor of Mabel Marie, though she often thought of them all. Hers had been a life of privilege, a far cry from the attic of the warehouse and the life she had so unexpectedly left behind. Olivia was lucky, for it had been only through the kindness and mercy of Sir Stanley that her life had changed so dramatically and now, at eighteen, a very different life lay ahead, one filled with possibilities.

"You are distracted today, Olivia," Lillian said, laying down her book and looking pointedly at Olivia, who was gazing out of the window.

"Oh, I am sorry, 'e, es, e, ons, ez, ent,' ... I think," Olivia said, repeating the French conjugation they had learned that morning, and blushing, as Lillian nodded.

"Fortunately, you have always been a quick learner, Olivia, and it is no wonder that you are distracted this morning, for I must confess that I am looking forward to his arrival too," Lillian said, closing the book of French grammar and smiling.

Arthur was due home from school that day for the summer. It had been almost three months since Olivia had last seen him, and she was excited to hear his news. They wrote to one another every week, but it was not the same as having him there, and she could not wait to tell him of all that had occurred since last they were together.

"I should make myself useful to Mrs. Mason. She was up at the crack of dawn to bake for Arthur's arrival," Olivia said, rising from her place at the table.

"Keep repeating the conjugations to yourself, make it almost like a song, 'e, es, e, ons, ez, ent,' and do so until you can think of nothing else," Lillian said, smiling at Olivia, who nodded.

"I think Arthur will be most impressed with my progress. I can certainly hold a conversation with him now," she said, and Lillian laughed.

"Do not forget the theatre tonight, perhaps you will wear your satin gown, the peacock blue one, you look so beautiful in that, Olivia," she said, and Olivia smiled.

"I will, and thank you," she said, as she left the room and hurried toward the kitchen where the delightful scent of baking wafted from the doorway.

Mrs. Mason was up to her elbows in dough, half a dozen cakes cooling on the side and trays of biscuits perched on almost every surface waiting for the oven. She looked up and smiled at Olivia, who took an apron from a hook by the door and rolled up her sleeves.

"Shall I make some jam tarts, Mrs. Mason? They are Arthur's favourite," she said, and the housekeeper laughed.

"I had forgotten the jam tarts; I knew there was something. Yes, that would be a great help, Olivia. I have some pastry spare over there and you may use any of the jam in the pantry, perhaps the apricot and the strawberry, yellow and red," she said.

Olivia rolled out the pastry as Mrs. Mason hummed to herself, putting the finishing touches to her loaves, which were now set to prove. It was always the same on the day of Arthur's return, the house filled with excitement and expectation as all was made ready.

"We are to go to the theatre tonight for a performance of *Twelfth Night*," Olivia said, as she began filling the pastry shells with jam.

"It is one of my favourites, I have seen it performed myself," Mrs. Mason replied, and Olivia looked at her in surprise.

"I did not know you liked Shakespeare, Mrs. Mason. In all the years I have known you, you have never mentioned it," Olivia said, and the housekeeper blushed.

"Well, what else do you think I do sat in this kitchen every evening? I have read the full works of Shakespeare, the tragedies and comedies, the histories and sonnets, they are beautiful," she replied, and Olivia smiled.

"Then we must talk of them, Mrs. Mason, for I am just in love with Shakespeare as you are, though I must confess I still have much to learn. I do not know *Twelfth Night* at all," she said, filling the last of the jam tarts.

"If music be the food of love, play on," Mrs. Mason said, in a most theatrical voice, one which Olivia had never heard her use before.

"From the play?" Olivia asked, smiling at the housekeeper, who nodded.

"Perhaps the most well-known. Oh, it is silly, but sometimes I imagine myself as an actress upon the stage. What a different life that would have been," she said, dusting down her apron.

"It is not silly at all, Mrs. Mason, it sounds to me like you know the plays better than anyone," Olivia said, but before Mrs. Mason could reply, a commotion in the hallway caused them both to let out a cry of delight.

"Master Arthur is here," Mrs. Mason cried, and the two of them rushed out into the hallways, as Sir Stanley emerged from his study and Lillian hurried from the drawing room.

One footman was just opening the door and out in the street, Olivia could see Arthur's carriage being unloaded, as he himself emerged onto the pavement.

"Arthur, Arthur!" Olivia cried, going to meet him at the door and throwing her arms around him.

"My dear Olivia, oh, how I have looked forward to this moment. Mother, Father, Mrs. Mason, how good it is to be home, I have missed you all," Arthur said.

He looked every bit the gentleman, dressed in tails and a top hat, breeches, and highly polished shoes, that ever-present and familiar smile upon his face, as he greeted them all one by one. Olivia felt somewhat embarrassed at the force of her greeting, but she was so happy to see him, so pleased to have her dearest friend back at her side after the long months of separation.

"Miss Olivia and I have been baking for the tea, Master Arthur. Your favourites," Mrs. Mason said, beaming at him, for she had always had a soft spot for Arthur.

"Jam tarts?" he asked, taking her by the hand, and Mrs. Mason nodded.

"Miss Olivia has made them herself, and there are cakes and biscuits, fresh bread and scones too," she said, and Arthur grinned.

"All my favourites, I must change and freshen up, for the journey has been tiring," he said, removing his hat and gloves, which Olivia took from him, before he hurried upstairs, returning a short while later dressed in a shirt and cravat, white breeches, and a waistcoat.

"We are to take tea in the drawing room now and tonight we are to attend the theatre," Olivia said, for she had waited in the hallway for his return.

He smiled at her and she blushed. It was always like this when Arthur returned from school, the excitement of anticipation replaced by a sense of embarrassment, though for what reason she could never be certain. Each time he returned, Arthur seemed to have grown, not only in stature but in wisdom and maturity. He was no longer the boy she had first met on that fateful day but a man, a gentleman, finding his way in the world and Olivia wondered what her own place in that world might be.

"I have so much to tell you, I can never fit it all into a letter. Perhaps after we have taken tea we might walk together in the park," he said, blushing, as he spoke.

Olivia smiled and nodded.

"I would like that very much, though I fear we have had few adventures here," she replied, as the two of them made their way into the drawing room.

Mrs. Mason had surpassed herself, a lavish tea laid out for them, the jam tarts sitting proudly in the centre.

"Come and sit down the two of you," Lillian said, as she and Sir Stanley smiled at them both.

"I have missed Mrs. Mason's teas, we are lucky if we get more than bread and butter at four o'clock," Arthur said, taking a plate and helping himself from the tea table.

Olivia held back, smiling at the sight of Arthur tucking into the jam tarts with exclamations of delight.

"Now, Arthur, you must tell us all that has happened at school this term. The last time you wrote you were about to sit your exams, I trust they were a success?" Sir Stanley asked, and Arthur nodded.

"Yes, Father, Mr. Dobbleson has suggested I may take the entrance exams for Oxford next year, if that is what you wish," Arthur replied, and his father smiled.

"Excellent, I shall write to the Master of Balliol, I see no reason to choose a different college from that of your father," Sir Stanley replied.

"But I have two friends who are seeking places at Exeter College, Father. I would be happier there. The chaplain is an old member of the school," Arthur said, reaching out for another jam tart and catching Olivia's eye as he did so.

"We shall see, you still have another year at the school, and I am sure all we can make the preparations," Sir Stanley replied.

"You are not the only one who has made excellent progress this term, Arthur," Lillian said, glancing at Olivia, who blushed.

"Ah, yes, of course, our resident French scholar, Dis-moi ce que tu as appris?" Arthur asked, and Olivia laughed.

"I have learned that I really know less than I thought," she replied, and Lillian tutted.

"You have done very well, Olivia, do not do yourself a discredit. Yesterday you translated a dozen pages of Victor Hugo without so much as a hint of assistance from me," she said, and Olivia nodded.

"I must confess, I enjoy my lessons, though I shall never be as fluent as you," she said, looking at Lillian, who smiled and shook her head.

"No, you shall be better," she replied, as the clock upon the mantelpiece struck five O'clock.

"Goodness me, if we are to make the theatre on time I must see to the last of my correspondence," Sir Stanley said, and the four of them rose.

"And Olivia and I shall take a walk in the park, the evening is too close to remain inside for its entire duration, I must have some air after the carriage ride," Arthur declared, and offering Olivia his arm, the two of them stepped out into the hallway and readied themselves for a walk.

***

It was a gentle summer evening, warm and inviting, the sweet scent of flowers wafting in the air, the trees in full bloom all around them. Arm in arm, they crossed the street and made their way along the wide walkway which spanned the park and where fashionable ladies and gentlemen were doing much the same. Arthur breathed in the fresh air and turned to Olivia with a smile.

"I have missed you," he said, and she blushed.

"And I have missed you too. The house is never quite the same without you, as much as I adore your mother and father," Olivia replied.

"They dote on you, you are just like a daughter to them," he said.

They were amongst the formal flower beds now, the roses sending up their sweet perfume, mixed with the smell of the box hedge, an ornamental fountain bubbling merrily in front of them. There were stone benches running all around the edge and Arthur invited Olivia to sit, the two of them enjoying the last of the afternoon sun.

"Do you think you will go to Oxford?" she asked, and he smiled.

"It is what my father wants, though I have no wish to go to Balliol, for they say there is no fun at Balliol. I am no scholar though, Olivia, even if I work hard," he replied, shaking his head.

"But you are the cleverest person I know, I have always thought it," she said, taking him by the hand.

"But there is more to life than just study, I wish for adventure, for excitement, and yet it appears my entire life is laid out for me. I shall enter business or worse, politics, for that is my father's ambition," he said.

"But what do you want?" she asked, and he looked up at her and smiled.

"For us always to be friends. Does that sound terribly foolish?" he replied, and Olivia was quite taken aback.

"I ... but of course not, there is nothing foolish is desiring friendship. We shall always be friends, you and I, of that I am certain," she said, and he shook his head sadly.

"You know I am to marry," he said, and Olivia nodded.

"I have heard your mother and father speaking of it," she replied, a heaviness coming over her heart, for the thought was a painful one.

"Granted there is no decision who it will be, but now my eighteenth birthday has passed the matter will soon be settled and a betrothal made. I cannot marry whilst a student at the university, but when those days of study are concluded, it is certain I shall do so. But Olivia, you must know something, you must know that if I were free to choose, then it would be you whom I would marry, if your feelings were the same," he said, causing Olivia to draw a sharp intake of breath.

Her feelings were the same, that much was true, for in the years of companionship and absence which they had shared, her heart had grown ever fonder of him. So much so that she knew her feelings could only be of love—and not that of a sister, but of one whose heart longed to be joined to the other, a love which could not be broken.

"But you know it is impossible," she replied, their hands now clasped together, a sad look in both their eyes.

"What foolish rules we find ourselves forced to live by. If my father were as much a radical as he claims, then he would tear them up," Arthur exclaimed, an angry tone entering his voice.

"Alas, it is not he who makes such rules. You cannot marry a servant, even one who speaks French and sits at table as your equal. I come from nowhere and have already far exceeded my true station in life. No, we must be content with the lot which is given us, though it be a sad burden to bear," Olivia replied, fighting back the tears in her eyes.

"It is a vain and foolish thing indeed," he said, shaking his head, "besides, I am to return to school at the end of the summer holidays and once again we must endure the sadness of separation."

"Let us be simply glad that fate has brought us together to enjoy the friendship which is ours," Olivia replied. "But come now, or we shall be late for the carriage to the theatre. Let us enjoy the evening and put these thoughts aside."

They made their way back through the park, arriving at the house just as the carriage drew up and Sir Stanley and Lillian emerged onto the steps.

"Oh, there you are, come along, do hurry, we shall be late," Sir Stanley called out, and Olivia and Arthur hurried to join them in the carriage.

It was only a quick journey to Covent Garden, and when they arrived outside the theatre a large crowd had already gathered. There was much excitement in the air and Sir Stanley led them inside the theatre, where they were shown to a box looking down upon the stage.

"What perfect seats," Olivia whispered, gazing down at the red plush curtains which would shortly open to reveal the stage.

"*Twelfth Night* is one of my favourite plays," Arthur said, as a waistcoated attendant served them glasses of claret.

"Did you know that Mrs. Mason is an admirer of Shakespeare?" Olivia asked, and Arthur laughed.

"Oh yes, she knows every play inside out. When I was a child, she used to tell me the stories whilst she got me ready for bed. She knew all the characters by heart. We should have invited her this evening," he said, turning to his father.

"I did," Sir Stanley replied, "but Mrs. Mason has quite old-fashioned views about the relationship between servants and their masters. She said it would not be appropriate for us all to be seen together, despite my considering Mrs. Mason as much a part of the family as you or Olivia."

"I shall take her back a programme, she will enjoy reading it, I am sure," Lillian said, just as a bell tinkled and the oil lamps around the theatre dimmed.

Olivia settled back for the performance, still with the thoughts of what Arthur had said going through her mind. There was no doubting the attraction between them, the innocence of childhood friendship having blossomed into something deeper and more profound. But despite their closeness, a barrier still lay between them, the barrier of birth and expectation, one which would forever keep them separated. How sad Olivia felt at the thought that she could never marry Arthur, not through any fault of their own, but because the world around them expected something different. Now, the curtains were drawn back, and a hush descended upon the theatre, as the actor stepped forth to begin the play.

"*If music be the food of love, play on; Give me excess of it, that, surfeiting,*

The appetite may sicken, and so die.

That strain again! it had a dying fall: O, it came o'er my ear like the sweet sound,

That breathes upon a bank of violets, Stealing and giving odour!

Enough; no more: 'Tis not so sweet now as it was before ..." he said, and Olivia was caught up in the delights of the play, the thought of love foremost in her mind.

Chapter 12
A Delightful Surprise

"And the way the actors spoke their lines, oh, Mrs. Mason, it was just wonderful," Olivia said, and the housekeeper laughed.

Olivia had spent much of the early morning extolling the delights of the performance in Covent Garden, as she and Mrs. Mason prepared the breakfast. She had hardly slept the night before, so entranced had she been by the performance. Theatre always had a similar effect upon her, more so in the company of Arthur. The two of them had spoken of little else as they journeyed home, and Olivia had risen early that morning to tell Mrs. Mason all about it.

"Such a beautiful story, I must read it again," Mrs. Mason said.

"You should have come with us, Sir Stanley offered for you to do so," Olivia said, as Mrs. Mason brought a tray of fresh breakfast rolls from the oven.

"I have said to Sir Stanley before that I am his housekeeper, not his confidant. I love this family, but I know my place in it," Mrs. Mason said, tutting, as she arranged the hot rolls in a basket.

"But you are part of the family, just as we all are," Olivia said, placing a pot of coffee on a tray and taking the basket of rolls.

"Sir Stanley treats you as a daughter and that is right and proper, Miss Olivia, but I must know my place," Mrs. Mason replied, pointing to the kitchen door. "Off you go with the tray, Master Arthur will be calling for his breakfast in a moment."

Olivia took the tray and made her way out into the hallway, just as Arthur came bounding down the stairs.

"I always sleep so well here. It must have been the play, or the fresh air or … the company," he said, smiling at Olivia, who blushed.

"The rolls are hot, just as you like them," she said, following him into the dining room, where Sir Stanley and Lillian were deep in conversation.

"Ah, Arthur, awake at last, sit down, will you," Sir Stanley said, and Arthur glanced at Olivia, the tone of Sir Stanley's voice sounding serious.

"Is something wrong, Father?" he asked, and Sir Stanley held up an official-looking letter, bearing a crest and embossed with a now broken wax seal.

"A letter from your school, at least what was your school," Sir Stanley said, and Arthur gave a start.

"But what do you mean, I left there only yesterday," he said, and his father raised his eyebrows.

"Well, it seems that there has been a mismanagement there these past months, a discrepancy in the finances. This letter is sent to inform me that the school will close, and they will seize its assets. It seems you will not be returning there in September as planned, though what that will mean for your education I do not know," Sir Stanley said, shaking his head, as Olivia poured out the coffee.

"But Father, they cannot just close the school, surely?" Arthur cried.

"If a school has no money, then it cannot function though the fees are high enough," Sir Stanley replied, as Arthur looked around in distress.

"But I have known nothing else. All my friends are there, and we had such plans for the final year. How will I get a place at Oxford now?" he cried, and Lillian hurried to comfort him.

"Do not worry, Arthur, we have a plan, your father does, at least," she said, as Olivia laid down the breakfast tray.

It upset her to see Arthur in such a state. Despite his claims to the contrary, Arthur was a most accomplished scholar and would surely go far, but with his school now closed there could be no hope of Oxford now.

"But what is it? I cannot go to another school," Arthur replied, his usual cheerful disposition now replaced by a sense of distress, as Sir Stanley took a deep breath.

"You shall remain here, and I shall employ a tutor to teach you. It is only a year until you go to Oxford and you would benefit from private tuition, I am sure. I will place an advertisement in *The Times,* and we shall ensure a first-rate tutor is employed to teach you," he said, words to which Arthur seemed visibly relieved.

"Then all is not lost," he said, and Sir Stanley shook his head.

"Not at all, and you shall still see your friends, for many of them live here in London," he said.

"And tell Olivia her good news too," Lillian said, and Olivia looked up in surprise.

Certainly, the thought of Arthur remaining at home with her was good news for them both, but what other happy fate might befall her that day?

"We have decided, Olivia, that since Arthur will be taught at home, we may as well see that you receive instruction, too. Now, obviously you have not had the complete schooling which he has, but you will most certainly benefit from further instruction and Lillian has suggested that she has taught you everything she is able," Sir Stanley said, as Olivia let out a cry of delight.

"You mean I am to learn alongside Arthur?" she said, the two of them looking at one another in delight.

"Indeed, for we are certain that with the right instruction you too can benefit from further education. I have always believed that the sex is no barrier to education, though I realise it is somewhat of a contentious point. Lillian has always worked to better herself and I believe you wish to do the same," he replied, as Olivia clapped her hands together in delight.

"When can we begin?" she asked, and Sir Stanley laughed.

"As soon as we find a suitable tutor. I shall have the advertisement placed immediately," he said, as Olivia and Arthur looked at one another in delight once more.

"Then there is some consolation in this sad news," he exclaimed, and it seemed to Olivia that there most certainly was.

***

Olivia and Arthur were hiding on the landing, just out of sight of the hallway. It was three days later, and Sir Stanley was down below, waiting for the first of the tutors who had responded to his advertisement. There had been dozens of replies, some more suitable than others, and Sir Stanley had chosen three, two men and a woman, to call for an interview. Olivia and Arthur had been delighted at the thought of learning together, though at the sight of the first candidate through the landing window, Olivia made a face.

"He looks rather stern," she said, as she and Arthur peered cautiously out.

The man was dressed in an academic gown and mortarboard, carrying what looked like a riding whip at his side, the sound of his heels clicking upon the path, as he strode toward the door before rapping loudly on the knocker.

"I do not think we would enjoy having this gentleman in our company," Arthur whispered, as the two of them turned back to the bannister and peered down.

"Ah, Mr. Craven?" Sir Stanley asked, as the footman opened the door, and they ushered in the gentleman.

"Mr. Craven, yes, Sir Stanley, and I will say from the outset that I am a man of discipline, a man of learning, and a man who takes no nonsense from anyone, least of all from children," he said, as Olivia and Arthur stifled a giggle.

"I … see," Sir Stanley replied, "will you step into my study, so that we might discuss matters further."

The door clicked behind them and Olivia and Arthur burst out laughing.

"I do not think that my father and Mr. Craven will see eye to eye on matters of education," Arthur said, and Olivia shook her head.

"Or on anything, for that matter," she replied.

The interview between Sir Stanley and Mr. Craven lasted for only a few minutes before the study door opened again and the sound of footsteps echoed across the hallway.

"I shall be in touch, Mr. Craven, until then, I wish you a good day," Sir Stanley said, as Olivia and Arthur peered through the bannisters.

"Spare the rod and spoil the child, Sir Stanley, that is the truth," Mr. Craven replied, and made his way to the door where the footman handed him his gloves.

As the door closed behind him, Olivia and Arthur stood up, and Sir Stanley glanced up, raising his eyebrows.

"No," he said, before stalking off into his study.

"The next one is due any moment, let us watch again from the window," Arthur said, and he and Olivia looked out, watching the gate through which a most extraordinary gentleman now appeared, wearing a turban, and swathed in multicoloured fabrics, walking with a gold topped cane.

"What an amazing sight," Olivia gasped as the gentleman approached the door and tapped lightly at the knocker.

"Professor Zingbani?" Sir Stanley could be heard saying, and Olivia and Arthur hurried to the bannister to catch a further glimpse of their next visitor.

He was a tall man, the turban adding extra height and Olivia now gazed at him open mouthed, for she had not noticed from the window that on his shoulder sat a monkey, happily counting its fingers and which now let out a shriek which caused Archibald and Marmaduke to dash up the stairs.

"I am Professor Zingbani, yes, and I am grateful to you, Sir Stanley, for inviting me to your home," he replied, his voice soft and with the slightest of accents to it.

"Indian, perhaps?" Arthur whispered, the two of them looking in amazement at the monkey who had now leapt down from his master's shoulder and was hopping around the hallway.

"Will you join me in my study?" Sir Stanley asked, and the professor bowed graciously.

"Come, Macalai, we must speak with Sir Stanley," he called out, and the monkey hopped obediently after him, as the door to the study closed.

"He would be marvellous," Arthur exclaimed, though the looks on the faces of Archibald and Marmaduke suggested differently.

"I wonder if he has any other animals?" Olivia speculated, and Arthur looked at her wide eyed.

"Snakes perhaps, or maybe a lion," he said, causing Olivia to recoil.

"I would not like that and certainly there is no room for a lion here. What would Mrs. Mason say?" she asked, and Arthur laughed.

"She would lock herself in the kitchen and never come out," he replied.

Suddenly, there came the sound of smashing crockery from below and the door to Sir Stanley's study opened and the monkey bounded out into the hallway. Further destruction now ensued, as the professor called desperately for him to stop.

"Macalai! Cease this," he cried, but the monkey appeared to have gone mad, and it was only the footman's flinging open of the door which brought an end to the destruction, as the monkey bounded out into the garden.

"I think we are perhaps not suited to having such a creature in the house," Sir Stanley could be heard saying, as the professor apologised profusely.

"Sir Stanley, a thousand pardons, I implore you and I will pay for the damage. It was the smell of the jam tarts you had upon the table, Macalai was raised upon them in India for they were my father, the Raj's favourites, and ever since he has had a taste for them," the professor replied, hurrying to the door.

"Then I think sadly we cannot welcome you here, for the absence of jam tarts would be a sadness for us all," Sir Stanley replied, and with a deep bow, the professor left the house.

As the door closed, Sir Stanley leant back upon it and pulled out a handkerchief to mop his brow. Olivia and Arthur peered once more over the bannister, and Sir Stanley looked up and laughed.

"He seemed jolly nice, Father," Arthur said, but Sir Stanley shook his head.

"A charming gentleman, but my study does not think so," he replied.

"Then what is to be done?" Arthur asked, and his father took out a pocketbook which he consulted, running his finger down the open page.

"Ah yes, Elizabeth Tupple, she is the last of the suitable candidates, though she does not arrive until later this afternoon. Enough time for me to get my study back in order. I only hope she is suitable, else we shall have to begin all over again. Goodness me, I never thought it would be so difficult to find a suitable tutor," he said, before returning to his study.

"Miss Tupple sounds awfully plain, not the sort with a monkey on her shoulder," Arthur said, and Olivia smiled.

"I am sure she will be terribly ordinary, but better that than the riding whip wielding Mr. Craven," she said, and the two of them made their way to the kitchen, drawn by the scent of fresh baking and the promise of the jam tarts which had so excited their exotic visitor.

Chapter 13
Miss Elizabeth Tupple

The clock had just struck four o'clock when the knock came at the door. Olivia and Arthur sat in the drawing room doing a puzzle and had quite forgotten about the last caller of the day. Each of them looked up in surprise.

"Oh, now we cannot see her," Arthur exclaimed, as Olivia made her way to the door, listening out for the sound of Sir Stanley emerging from his study to welcome their visitor.

"Miss Tupple?" he could be heard asking.

"Lady Tupple, Sir Stanley, my mother and father are Lord and Lady Artemis Tupple of Kent, my father has just inherited the Earldom, now that my grandfather has passed away," came the reply.

"A lady of some importance," Olivia whispered, as Arthur came to join her at the door.

"Ah, I had not realised, your response to the advertisement gave no indication," Sir Stanley exclaimed.

"Forgive me, but I prefer not to dwell upon titles and privileges. I have always wanted to be a governess or, in this case, a tutor, and I assure you I have all the requisite learning to prepare your son for Oxford," she replied, as Olivia and Arthur continued to listen at the door.

"Then step this way, Lady Tupple, we shall discuss the matter further. I know of your mother and father, of course. Your father's reputation is formidable," Sir Stanley said, as the door closed behind them.

"She seems delightful," Olivia said, and Arthur nodded.

"Though somewhat shy, perhaps," he said, and the two of them returned to their puzzle.

It was almost half an hour later when the door to the study was heard to open and Sir Stanley's voice echoed in the hallway.

"My wife will be eager to meet you, Lady Tupple, as will Arthur and Olivia. Please, taking a seat in the morning room and I will call for some refreshment," he said, and they could hear Elizabeth thanking him.

A moment later, the drawing-room door opened, and Sir Stanley appeared, smiling broadly.

"You have made your decision, Father?" Arthur asked, and Sir Stanley nodded.

"She is perfect, you will both be enamoured of her, I am certain of it," he replied, rubbing his hands together gleefully.

"And she is of aristocratic stock?" Arthur continued, and his father raised his eyebrow.

"Arthur, is there any need to ask questions when you have listened in on the entire conversation?" he said, and Arthur blushed.

"Only the first part," he admitted.

"Quickly now, ready yourselves and then come to meet her, I will call your mother," Sir Stanley said, leaving the room and calling out for Mrs. Mason to bring tea and jam tarts to the morning room.

"Come then, Olivia, we must be polite," Arthur said, and the two of them hurried out into the hallway.

"I must just get a shawl from upstairs, my shoulders are cold," Olivia said, and she dashed upstairs, returning just as Mrs. Mason was emerging from the kitchen with a tray of tea and treats.

"I wonder if she is a lover of Shakespeare, Miss Olivia?" Mrs. Mason said, making her way into the morning room, where the sound of voices echoing out into the hallway could be heard.

Olivia paused for a moment, feeling almost embarrassed at the thought of meeting Lady Tupple. Even now, after all these years of living with Sir Stanley and his family, she found herself still torn between two worlds. She did not consider herself to have those aristocratic tendencies which came naturally to the others and at dinners and parties she shied away from conversation, preferring to stay close to Lillian or Arthur and doubting herself to be an object of interest.

"Come in, Olivia, we are waiting for you," Lillian said, peering around the door and startling Olivia, who nodded and glanced a final look in the hallway mirror, pulling the shawl around her shoulders.

Mrs. Mason had just poured out the tea, a china cup held delicately in Elizabeth's hands, and she was speaking with Sir Stanley, who had just introduced her to Arthur. Olivia entered the room and Elizabeth looked up, a smile upon her face which turned immediately to a look of utter astonishment, as she let out a cry and dropped her teacup. The cup smashed upon the floor and there was much profuse apology by Lady Tupple, who continued to stare at Olivia, who returned her gaze in surprise.

"Please, accept my apologies, I am ever so clumsy, how silly of me," she exclaimed, as Mrs. Mason tutted and knelt to pick up the pieces of smashed crockery.

"Lady Tupple, are you all right? You are as white as a ghost," Lillian said, and Elizabeth nodded.

"Forgive me, it is just … you are Olivia?" she asked, looking intensely at Olivia, who nodded.

"Yes," Olivia replied, blushing under Lady Tupple's gaze.

"Extraordinary," she whispered, as much to herself as to the company.

"Is something wrong, Lady Tupple? Olivia has been a daughter to us these many years, just as I explained," Sir Stanley said.

"There is nothing wrong, merely a most remarkable likeness, a coincidence, please, I would not dwell upon it. Tell me, both of you, what have you learned and what do you desire to learn?" she asked, though Olivia could not help but remain puzzled by what had just occurred.

They took tea together and Olivia and Arthur both gave accounts of their learning and of what they hoped to achieve, which, for Olivia, was quite different to Arthur. Nevertheless, Lady Tupple assured them both that she would do all she could to help Arthur achieve his ambitions for a place at Oxford and Olivia her own of learning all she could and of being a help to Sir Stanley in his work.

"Then we shall expect you upon Sunday, your rooms shall be prepared, and the lessons will begin on Monday morning," Sir Stanley said, as they concluded their tea and the family bid Lady Tupple good day.

"It has been a delight to meet you all and I look forward to beginning our work together very much," Lady Tupple said, taking them each by the hand.

But when she came to Olivia, an odd look came over her and she shook her head, as though unable to believe something her mind was telling her.

"You are a very beautiful young lady," she said, and Olivia blushed.

"Thank you, Lady Tupple, for I would not presume to believe it myself," she replied.

"You take after your mother perhaps," she replied, and Olivia shook her head.

"I never knew my mother, so I cannot answer truthfully or deny it," she said, and Lady Tupple smiled.

"I am sure you do," she said, and with that, she wished them all a pleasant afternoon.

"There now, we are fortunate to have discovered such a woman, I am certain of it," Sir Stanley said, as the door closed behind Lady Tupple and he turned to the family and smiled.

"What came over her when she saw Olivia?" Arthur asked.

"It was as though she had seen a ghost," Lillian said, looking at Olivia in astonishment.

"I do not know … though I fear I may be able to guess," Olivia said, and the others looked at her in surprise.

"What do you mean?" Lillian asked, as Olivia blushed.

"Well, in the time before, when I lived with Mr. Gobler, sometimes it was … convenient to take advantage of ladies such as her. They would leave their purses and bags open at their sides, and it was easy for a girl such as I to get close to them and steal. I am not proud of it, but no doubt she recognises me from such an incident, even though it was always too late to stop me from getting away," Olivia said, and Lillian patted her arm.

"Those days are long gone now, Olivia. It matters not if that is the case. Lady Tupple will know what a fine and upstanding young lady you have turned out to be. Now, I must see to her chambers, there is an awful lot to do if we are to be ready by Sunday," she said, bustling off, just as Archibald and Marmaduke appeared at the top of the stairs.

Arthur and Sir Stanley had business to discuss, and so Olivia made her way into the kitchen where she found Mrs. Mason plucking pheasants for a pie. The housekeeper looked up and smiled as Olivia sat down heavily at the table and put her head in her hands.

"Now what is wrong, Olivia, my dear?" Mrs. Mason asked, holding up the half-plucked bird and plucking further feathers from its breast.

"Lady Tupple recognised me, and I do not know why," Olivia said, shaking her head.

"She has probably confused you with someone else. These women meet so many people that it is hardly surprising," Mrs. Mason said, the remnants of the smashed china cup lying on a tray on the table.

"But she was so surprised. You saw the look on her face. It was more than recognition, it was shock," Olivia said, looking up at the housekeeper who laid down the pheasant and came to put her arm around her.

"Do not fret, Miss Olivia. If Lady Tupple has seen something strange in you, then I am sure she will make herself clear. Remember, she will be just as nervous about coming here to teach you and Master Arthur, as you are of having someone new in the house. I know you are wary of strangers," Mrs. Mason said, and Olivia smiled.

"You know me too well, Mrs. Mason, you really do," she replied, and the housekeeper laughed.

"Come now, help me with these pies, else none of us shall eat tonight," she said, and Olivia rolled up her sleeves and took up a rolling pin to make the pastry cases.

But try as she might, Olivia could not rid herself of the memory of Lady Tupple's look. It seemed so astonished, as though she had recognised her from some past encounter, one which Olivia did not wish to be reminded of. She had largely forgotten her old life, preferring to concentrate upon the new; her mind turned to the future and not the past. But now it seemed she would be forced to confront a ghost from the time before, one which might raise further the spectres of the past and spoil her chances of happiness forever.

Chapter 14
At Home with Arthur

Lady Tupple arrived as arranged on Sunday afternoon. She came in a carriage, accompanied by several enormous trunks, and was greeted by Sir Stanley and Lillian before once again being introduced to Arthur and Olivia. Gone was her look of wide-eyed shock and disbelief, replaced by a friendly and delightful demeanour and the promise that the three of them would soon be the best of friends.

"You shall take your lessons together, of course, but I shall tailor our curriculum to suit each of you individually. For example, Olivia will concentrate upon her French, whilst Arthur will continue his close studies of Latin and Greek. Those are the languages of the universities and we must do all we can to prepare you for Balliol," she said, as they sat taking tea together.

"Exeter," Arthur replied, grinning at his father, who let out a snort.

"So long as you get your place, that is all that matters," Sir Stanley replied, and Lady Tupple smiled.

"I will do all I can to help, Sir Stanley, but it must be Arthur who works for it," she said.

"And you will be pleased to hear Olivia's progress upon the pianoforte," Lillian said, smiling at Olivia, who blushed.

"You play the pianoforte? Oh, how delightful that is. My sister ... God rest her soul, for she died many years ago, was an accomplished player. I used to sit and listen to her for hours. She was older than I, and I idolised her. It would be a pleasure to hear you play," she said, and Olivia nodded.

"I will gladly do so," she replied.

In the days since she had first encountered Lady Tupple, Olivia's own worries had lessened. No longer did she fear what connection there might be between herself and the tutor, for Lillian was right, the events of the past were no longer of relevance and she could hold her head up proudly as a person who had changed their ways and made the best of their life. She was no street urchin anymore, but the adopted daughter of Sir Stanley Evans, an upright and respectable man who, along with his wife, had turned her into a respectable lady.

"Then I look forward to it. I am certain that the three of us will get along very well. I am not much older than you, fourteen years, I believe, and I am sure that many of our tastes will be the same," Lady Tupple said, beaming at them all.

She was a pretty woman, or so Olivia thought, with black hair combed into a bob and rosy red cheeks, ample in figure, though not ungainly, and with such delightful mannerisms that Olivia warmed to her already. The initial shock of their first encounter was gone, replaced now hoping Lady Tupple could teach her much she did not know, as well as be a new and interesting companion.

"I hope the chambers we have prepared are suitable for you, Lady Tupple. They are at the top of the house, a sitting room and a bedroom, looking out over the gardens at the back," Lillian said, and Elizabeth smiled.

"They will do perfectly well, thank you. I should very much like to see them," she said, and Mrs. Mason was called to show her upstairs.

"A delightful woman, I think she will be a great asset to us all," Sir Stanley said, when Lady Tupple had left the drawing room.

"Did you ever work out why she was so shocked to see you?" Arthur asked, as he and Olivia made their way out into the hallway, but Olivia shook her head.

"I can only imagine it must have been some dreadful incident from the past, one which I would rather forget and which she is too polite to mention again," Olivia said, smiling at him.

"I am sure it is nothing. Come along, we have time for a walk in the park before dinner. Shall we see if the lilies are out in the ornamental gardens?" he asked, offering her his hand.

***

They had now turned the nursery into something of a school room, the toys and rocking horse replaced with several desks and a large chalkboard, along with an enormous globe which showed the extent of the British Empire. Many charts and tables were upon the walls, and a bookcase contained several weighty tomes, along with the classics of current literature and textbooks of language, science, and history. Olivia and Arthur were waiting patiently for Lady Tupple, the clock upon the wall having just passed nine o'clock and the two of them having taken an early breakfast a short while before.

"e, es, e, ons, ez, ent," Olivia was repeating to herself, making Arthur laugh.

"If I hear you recite that one more time, then I shall surely forget all the Latin declensions in my mind," he said, and Olivia blushed.

"I just want to get it right, that is all," she replied, as the door to the nursery opened and Lady Tupple hurried in, carrying a stack of books precariously in front of her.

"Someone should chastise me for my tardiness, a hundred apologies to you both. Now, let me see," she said, laying down the books and taking up a piece of chalk.

She turned to the blackboard and wrote in large, spidery letters.

'Lady Elizabeth Tupple, of Kent.'

"It is a lovely name," Olivia said, and Arthur nodded.

"But forgive me, Olivia, I do not know your second name, or have you adopted that of Sir Stanley?" Elizabeth asked, and Olivia looked at Arthur and blushed.

"I … I do not know my name, only Olivia," she replied, "but in circumstances I am taken for the daughter of Sir Stanley, so I suppose Olivia Stanley is my name now."

"No name? But tell me, Olivia, where did you come from? Sir Stanley has told me a little of the circumstances, but I know very little of you, far less than I do of Arthur," she said.

"There is little to tell, Lady Tupple. I am an orphan and I was taken to an orphanage as a baby, though of course I can remember nothing of it, and from there I eventually escaped to London. I lived for many years with a group of street urchins under the direction of a Mr. Gobler. We were pickpockets, until they decided that this very house should make a tempting target," Olivia replied, shaking her head.

"And that is when she became as a sister to me," Arthur said, grinning.

"And you have lived here ever since? But have you never been curious as to your true identity, Olivia? Never wondered who your parents were or where you came from?" Elizabeth asked, and Olivia shrugged her shoulders.

"I know I shall never find the answer and so I have given up such a search. Besides, I have a family here, one whom I love with all my heart and would never wish to give up, even if by some miracle I were to find the truth as to my lineage," Olivia replied, and Lady Tupple smiled.

"You speak with great sincerity, Olivia. Now, we should begin, first some Latin for you, Arthur, I have a wonderful poem here for you to translate and for you, Olivia, a piece of French prose which I think you will very much enjoy. After that, we shall take a music lesson, for I would so very much like to hear you play, Olivia," she said, opening two books and passing them to Olivia and Arthur, respectively.

They spent a happy hour about their translations and then made much merriment in reciting them to Lady Tupple, each much to the amusement of the other.

"The snow is fled: the trees their leaves put on, the fields their green: earth owns the change, and rivers lessening run

their banks between. *Naked the Nymphs and Graces in the meads,"* Arthur began, and Olivia giggled at the pompous manner in which he spoke.

"And why is it funny, might I ask? Naked Nymphs are in almost every portrait hanging in the National Gallery," Arthur replied, sounding indignant.

"Horace certainly has a way with words," Lady Tupple said, raising her eyebrows and smiling.

"It is the way you say it, not the words themselves," Olivia replied, for she had never heard Arthur speaking in such a formal manner.

He pursed his lips at her, before sniggering, the two of them falling about laughing as Elizabeth clapped her hands.

"Now, now, I think we shall skip hearing Olivia's French. Come, let us go down to the morning room and hear Olivia play the pianoforte," she said, and the three of them left the nursery, entering the morning room, just as Mrs. Mason was bringing in coffee for Lillian.

"Ah, Mrs. Mason, will you stay and hear Olivia play for us?" Elizabeth asked, but Mrs. Mason only laughed.

"I have heard her often enough, Lady Tupple and if I were to stand listening to her every time she sat down to play, then there would never be a meal served in this house," she said, setting down the coffee and smiling at Olivia, who stifled a laugh.

"Well, we shall listen to her, if we are not disturbing you?" Lady Tupple replied, turning to Lillian, who shook her head and smiled.

"Not at all, I love to hear Olivia play. She has become remarkably adept. It is surely a natural talent upon her part, for I have done little to teach her. My ability is somewhat lacking," she said, as Olivia settled herself down at pianoforte and wondered what to play.

She had been learning a new piece of Bach, one which she was having trouble in perfecting, though she was determined to get right, eventually. The music lay open on the stand in front of her and she ran her fingers across the keys, the notes tinkling in the air, as Arthur and Lady Tupple settled themselves down by the window.

"The food of love," Arthur said, smiling at her.

"Do you know Shakespeare well?" Elizabeth asked, and both of them nodded.

"Our entire household knows him well, even Mrs. Mason," Olivia said, her hands poised over the keys.

"When you are ready, Olivia," Lady Tupple said, and Olivia began to play.

The presence of an audience was enough to focus her mind, causing her to concentrate on each note and avoiding the mistakes which had dogged her when last she had practiced the piece. It seemed to come easily to her now, each note following the previous in perfect harmony. How she delighted in the sound, filled with delight at having at last accomplished what she had believed to have been impossible to perfect.

As the music ended, she looked up and was amazed to see Elizabeth in tears, sobbing, her cheeks flushed. Lillian took out a handkerchief and handed it to Lady Tupple, who dabbed her eyes and apologised. Having composed herself, she clapped, beaming at Olivia, who turned the page to play again.

"Another piece, perhaps?" she asked, and Lady Tupple shook her head.

"Forgive me, your playing was exquisite, Olivia, you bring back memories of my dear sister. She was ever so accomplished upon the pianoforte, just as you are. There is something about the way you play that reminds me of her, it is simply remarkable. Oh, goodness me, I am all of a flutter," she said, dabbing at her eyes again.

"Perhaps a turn in the garden would do you good, Lady Tupple," Lillian said, and Elizabeth nodded.

"I think so, if you would excuse me for just a moment," she said, and with a final tearful glance at Olivia, she hurried from the room.

"You have certainly made an impression upon our guest," Lillian said, as Olivia looked at her and Arthur in surprise.

"She is right, though. Your playing is exquisite, Olivia," Arthur said, causing Olivia to blush.

"I had not perfected that piece until today. The notes had alluded me, the right ones, at least. But with an audience, well, it appeared I had to get it right," she said, glancing down at the open music, still amazed at the reaction she had caused in Lady Tupple.

"She speaks often of her sister," Arthur said, "I wonder what sad tragedy befell her, childbirth perhaps. That causes the sad demise of those of our rank and class, the women at least."

"She bears some heavy burden, that much is certain," Lillian said, shaking her head sadly.

Olivia was puzzled. First there had been the extraordinary reaction of Lady Tupple on the first day of their meeting and now this same outpouring of emotion before the pianoforte. Was it simply the music or could it be Olivia herself? Her playing having evoked something deep within Lady Tupple to rouse memories long suppressed.

"I wonder if we shall ever know what it is," Arthur mused, and his mother tutted.

"It is not for us to wish to know such things, Arthur. If she carries some pain or tragedy with her, then that is not for us to think upon, but for her to speak of if she so wishes. Now, I am sure you both wish to return to your lessons," Lillian said, as the sound of the door in the hallway opening could be heard and Lady Tupple called out for them both to join her.

Back in the nursery, they resumed their translation work, but Olivia could not help but keep glancing at Elizabeth, wondering again what she kept hidden. When would Olivia display by chance some reminder of Lady Tupple's sister, bringing forth a fresh burst of emotion? She was a mystery to her, an enigma, and a secret, concealing something in which Olivia saw herself caught up. It was most strange and, when the lessons were concluded, Elizabeth called for Olivia to hold back, as Arthur hurried from the nursery, keen to enjoy the sun in the garden.

"You really played so beautifully this morning, Olivia," she said, and Olivia blushed.

"It was Lillian who taught me, she does not take credit well enough for having done so," Olivia replied.

"Ah, but there must be some natural talent there, an inheritance, surely," Elizabeth replied, but Olivia only shook her head.

"It does not feel natural when I have to practice so hard to give only the merest hint of a decent performance," she said.

"My sister never believed in her own abilities, but I did. I thought the world of her," Elizabeth said, smiling at Olivia, who blushed.

"She must have been a delightful person," Olivia replied, and Elizabeth nodded.

"She was, but sadly … she was lost. I must not keep you though, Olivia, go and spend time with Arthur, the two of you are made for one another," she said, and Olivia blushed an even deeper shade of red.

"Oh, you do not understand, we are not … we cannot be," she said, and Elizabeth appeared embarrassed.

"Oh, I am sorry, forgive me," she said, and an awkward silence now descended upon them.

Olivia excused herself, hurrying out into the garden, where she found Arthur drinking lemonade under the large beech tree which grew in the corner.

"Lady Tupple had mistaken us for … more than simply friends," Olivia said, coming to sit down next to him, and Arthur laughed.

"If only more would do so, then perhaps we would not have such difficulties," he said, picking up a fallen twig and tossing it across the lawn.

"Perhaps if I work hard, truly better myself," she began, but Arthur only shook his head.

"It is only a matter of time before I am found a wife, of that I am certain. Despite that, we can enjoy our time together now, can we not?" he said, and Olivia smiled.

"We shall always enjoy our time together, Arthur. Whatever fate has in store for us," she said, settling herself down next to him, as he handed her a glass of lemonade.

***

"The Scottish Play, or so they call it, for it is bad luck to mention the name," Sir Stanley said, holding up an advertisement at the breakfast table.

It had been two weeks since Lady Tupple had arrived to live with them, and in that time, she had settled in well. There had been no further outbursts of emotion and she and Olivia had grown close, each confiding in the other, so that it felt to Olivia as though she had gained an elder sister.

"We must attend the performance, it will be simply wonderful. Do you know the play, Mrs. Mason?" Lillian asked, as the housekeeper entered the dining room with dish of sausages in hand.

"I know it is a bloody tale, ma'am, and does not end particularly well for anyone," she said, causing Sir Stanley to laugh.

"And you must come to see it with us, Mrs. Mason. Please now, I insist," he said, causing the housekeeper to roll her eyes.

"Oh, Sir Stanley, you know I know my place well enough, I cannot possibly accompany you," she replied.

"You are part of my family, Mrs. Mason and I insist. If you do not, then … then … then I shall never eat another of your jam tarts so long as I live," he said, causing Arthur to startle.

"Father, you cannot mean it," he cried, and Sir Stanley nodded.

"I mean it, I certainly do. Not another one of Mrs. Mason's delectable jam tarts will pass my lips if she refuses to accompany us to the theatre tonight. My suffering will be hers too, for she will have only you to make them for and when you leave for Oxford, this house will be bereft of her jam tarts forever," he said, sounding terribly solemn, so that Mrs. Mason let out a heavy sigh.

"Oh, very well, Sir Stanley, you shall have your way, I will come to the theatre with thanks, but I will feel terribly uncomfortable sat in a fancy box and with all eyes upon me," she said, shaking her head.

"I will help you find something wonderful to wear, Mrs. Mason," Olivia said, and Sir Stanley smiled.

"Excellent, and you too, Lady Tupple, I trust you will accompany us?" he said, and Lady Tupple nodded.

"It would be my pleasure, Sir Stanley. The Scottish Play is one of my favourites and it is a long time since last I saw it performed," she replied.

"Excellent, then it appears we all to have a most enjoyable evening," Sir Stanley said, as the family rose from the breakfast table, Archibald and Marmaduke eyeing the uneaten dish of sausages with hungry expressions.

***

There were to be no lessons that day, for it was Saturday and Olivia and Arthur spent the day in the garden, enjoying the sunshine and reading to one another. It pleased Olivia to read to Arthur, a token of her gratitude for the hours he had spent doing so for her when they were younger. She was reading a work by Mr. Dickens, telling the story of a boy called David Copperfield and his adventures.

"Quite remarkable, I wish my own life had been such as his," Arthur said, rolling on his back and gazing up into the sky above.

"I think you have a rather romantic view of what constitutes adventure, Arthur," Olivia said, for he had called her own exploits adventures, when she considered them more ordeals than excitement.

"But my own life has always seemed so dull compared to those I read of. To run away to sea or to be caught up in battle, what I would not give for that," Arthur said, his voice sounding wistful.

"I think you would prefer it less if it were truly happening to you," she replied, and he laughed.

"Perhaps you are right. Still, it is nice to dream," he said.

"And is not the theatre a chance to put yourself into such feelings, to live adventure through the eyes of others?" she asked, closing the book as Arthur sat up.

"True, very true," he said, as she rose to her feet.

"Now, I must help Mrs. Mason. She will be all a fluster and I must look for a dress for myself. I have been so very hot these past few days, something light," she said, and smiling at him, she hurried off across the garden and let herself in at the kitchen door.

Mrs. Mason was, as Olivia expected, in a state of some nervous excitement, wringing her hands and shaking her head, as Olivia entered the kitchen.

"Oh, I do not know what to wear. Look, the mistress has offered me three outfits, though which is best I do not know. You must choose for me, Olivia," she said, pointing at the three dresses which were hung by the door.

One was peacock blue, another red, and there was a plain white dress, too, edged with a lace trim. They were each of them beautiful and would all have fitted Mrs. Mason well, for she was an attractive woman, though she disguised it well beneath a plethora of petticoats and aprons.

"The peacock blue would suit you very well, Mrs. Mason," Olivia said, taking it down from its hanging and holding it up to the housekeeper who blushed.

"But I do not wish to appear better dressed than you ladies," she said, causing Olivia to laugh.

"And why ever not? There is no crime in dressing well, Mrs. Mason. I doubt you will ever accept an invitation like this again, so resolute are you in your convictions. Wear the blue and look like the lady you are," Olivia said, causing Mrs. Mason to laugh.

"Well, if you insist, Miss Olivia, I will. Have you chosen your own dress yet? You have so many pretty ones," Mrs. Mason said, still looking warily at the blue dress, as though any desire for fashion was not proper for a housekeeper.

"Anything that will prevent the heat of the theatre from making me faint," Olivia replied, and Mrs. Mason laughed.

"But you must take a shawl in that case, for these summer nights can still be cold, particularly if we shall wait for the carriage after the performance," she said.

Olivia smiled and hurried off upstairs to get ready. She had little difficulty in choosing a dress, opting for one which

Sir Stanley had bought for her the previous year as a birthday present. It was shoulderless, yet with long sleeves and a tasteful bust, peach and made of satin, with sequins and lace trim, the perfect summer outfit. The evening was warm, though she heeded Mrs. Mason's advice and wrapped herself in a shawl.

It took an hour to get ready, and the clock had just struck six o'clock when she finished her preparations and made her way downstairs. Arthur was waiting there, dressed now in tails and a frock coat, a handsome waistcoat beneath and a cravat at the neck. He looked terribly handsome and Olivia could not help but feel a shiver of delight run through her at the sight of him holding out his arm to escort her.

"You look beautiful, Olivia," he said, and she blushed.

"And so does Mrs. Mason," Lillian declared, stepping from the kitchen doorway, as Mrs. Mason followed nervously behind.

Except that it was not Mrs. Mason at all who stood before them, but a radiant vision of what the housekeeper truly could be. Gone was the flour covered apron, the layers of petticoats and the tied back hair, replaced by an elegant woman in a beautiful blue dress, her hair combed up into a bouffant and long silk gloves upon her hands reaching up to her elbows. It was a remarkable sight and Olivia and Arthur let out a cry of delight, rushing to embrace her.

"You see, I told you how pretty you would look, I told you," Olivia said, kissing the housekeeper upon both cheeks, as she blushed.

"I never thought I could look like this, never in all my wildest dreams," she said, as Sir Stanley emerged from his study.

"Where is my housekeeper, what impostor is this?" he asked, bowing low, and taking Mrs. Mason's hand, bringing it to his lips and causing her to giggle.

"Oh, Sir Stanley," she said, glancing at Lillian, who laughed.

"You deserve every accolade, Mrs. Mason. Come now, we must go," she said.

"What of Lady Tupple? Ought not we to wait for her?" Arthur exclaimed, and Sir Stanley nodded.

"Of course, I had quite forgotten her. And the two of you, you both look very smart, my dear Olivia, that is a beautiful dress," he said, and Olivia smiled.

Just then, there came a footfall upon the stairs above and Lady Tupple appeared, resplendent in a gold gown and silver sash, sweeping down the stairs and greeting them with open arms.

"Is there anything more exciting than the theatre? Story, adventure, excitement, all mixed into one," she said, beaming at them.

"You look beautiful, Lady Tupple," Sir Stanley said, and she curtsied.

"You are too kind, Sir Stanley. I wore this for my eighteenth birthday and I am proud to say, that all these years later it still fits," she said, smiling at Olivia.

"And you wear it very well," Lillian said, as the sounds of a carriage drawing up could be heard from outside.

"Ah, here we are, the carriage awaits," Sir Stanley said, offering Lillian his arm,

"Might I?" Arthur asked, offering his to Olivia, who nodded.

"But first, I must take off this shawl it is far too warm," she said, removing the shawl and handing it to Mrs. Mason, who, ever practical, had brought with her a bag.

But as she removed the shawl, exposing her shoulders, Lady Tupple screamed and fainted to floor, Sir Stanley rushing to her side.

"Goodness me, bring smelling salts. Arthur, summon the footmen. What terrible shock is this? Lady Tupple, please speak to us," Sir Stanley cried, trying to revive Lady Tupple, who lay motionless on the hallway floor.

There was much commotion and back and forth, before Lady Tupple was carried into the drawing room and laid upon the chaise lounge by the window which was opened to allow fresh air to enter the room, for it was stuffy and warm. Gradually, with the aid of smelling salts and a glass of cold water, Lady Tupple was revived. The family stood over her with concern, as she blinked and looked up.

"Lady Tupple, are you all right?" Lillian asked, and Lady Tupple took a deep gulp of air, attempting to sit up.

"Now, now, you have had a shock, Lady Tupple, lie back now and rest," Sir Stanley said, but Lady Tupple would not be dissuaded, and she sat up, looking straight at Olivia, and pointing.

"Olivia, what is that?" she asked, and Olivia looked at her in surprise.

"What is what?" she asked, and Lady Tupple narrowed her eyes.

"That, on your upper arm," she said, and Olivia looked down in surprise.

"Merely a birth mark, Lady Tupple. I rarely wear dresses such as this, but it is so warm this evening that I could not bear the thought of sitting in the theatre in a heavy dress," she said, as Lady Tupple beckoned her forward.

"It cannot be any other, it cannot be," she said, half to herself and half to the others.

"What do you mean, Lady Tupple? What has Olivia's birth mark to do with your current excitable state?" Sir Stanley asked, sounding thoroughly confused.

"Because now there is no doubt in my mind who Olivia is. I thought it could be, I wondered if it could be, I wanted it to be, I longed for it to be, and now I know," she said, tears welling up in her eyes.

Olivia was confused. She had only known Lady Tupple for a few weeks and there was no suggestion that they had known one another previously. She looked from Sir Stanley, to Lillian, to Arthur, and Mrs. Mason, astonished at Elizabeth's words.

"But who do you think I am?" Olivia asked, and Lady Tupple smiled.

"You are my niece, Olivia," she said, and now it was Olivia's turn to faint.

Chapter 15
An Extraordinary Revelation

When Olivia came round, she found Arthur looking down at her, a smile upon his face. He held a glass of water to her mouth, from which she took a sip, blinking in the evening sunshine coming through the window. They had placed her in a chair and Lillian was fanning her gently, the cool air a welcome relief from the heat she felt surging through her, her head feeling light and airy.

"How long …" she asked, recalling the astonishing words which had led to her current position.

"Only a few minutes, I caught you before you fell to the floor," he replied, as Olivia sat up.

Lady Tupple had a large glass of brandy in her hand and sat upon the chaise lounge, a look of utter astonishment upon her face.

"Are we all done with fainting?" Sir Stanley asked, and both women nodded.

"Then we must know the facts," Arthur said, as Lady Tupple took a sip of brandy.

"I knew it just as soon as I saw Olivia on that first day. I said to myself, 'it must be her,' but I had no proof of it, it was only the look and the name too, of course. But there are many Olivia's and just because she has my sister's look to her, that was no reason to upset her by declaring it. When she played the pianoforte, I came to suspect it again. There was something in the way she played, so natural, so beautiful. But what would I have done? Told her of my suspicions? It would hardly be proper. But now I know, in absolute certainty, I know," Elizabeth said, looking up and smiling at Olivia, who still could not take it all in.

"The birthmark?" she whispered, and Lady Tupple nodded.

"That is right, the birth mark, the same birth mark I saw on the shoulder of my niece on the night that she was born. My sister – your mother – met a dreadful end, for she died shortly after you were born of terrible complications," Lady Tupple said, pulling out a handkerchief and dabbing at her eyes.

But Olivia was confused. If she was the daughter of a woman such as Lady Tupple described, then why was she sent away as she was, abandoned at an orphanage, instead of taken care of by the grandparents whom Elizabeth had spoken of so often in the previous weeks?

"But I do not understand. Where is my father? Surely my mother was married to a man of noble standing, if what you say is true," Olivia continued, but Lady Tupple shook her head.

"Alas, the tale is a sad and sorry one, Olivia. Your father was but an undergardener upon the estate, though your mouther loved him dearly. My father would never have allowed them to marry and when the indis– when it was discovered that she was with child, they sent him away, never to be heard of again. The scandal was too great, and they hid your birth from the world. No one knew save my parents, myself, and our faithful nursemaid, no one else," Elizabeth said.

"And you are certain of all this?" Olivia asked, for she had no desire to be hurt by these revelations, or to fall into a trap.

"As certain as I have even been of anything, Olivia. Your name, your circumstances, your looks, and now this. But wait, I can show you," she said, and she reached into her pocket and brought out a locket.

It was made of gold, inlaid with pearl, and Elizabeth opened it, revealing the portrait of a woman, a woman with the most striking resemblance to Olivia.

"But it is you," Arthur gasped, as the family peered down at the miniature, the woman's face smiling back.

"My mother," Olivia whispered, and Elizabeth nodded.

"Lady Beatrice Tupple, my dearest and sweetest friend, the one I long for everyday," she replied, as a tear ran down her cheek.

"What a beautiful name," Lillian said, reaching out and taking Olivia's hand in hers and squeezing it.

"I … I do not know what to say," Olivia replied.

All her life she had wondered who her mother was, imagined her to be like this or like that. She had given up all hope of ever finding her, of ever knowing her, of ever discovering the truth about where she came from. Now, entirely by chance and good fortune, she had discovered the truth, or rather, the truth had discovered her. It seemed almost too much to take in, and she sighed, putting her head into her hands, as tears welled up in her eyes.

"It is like finding my sister, for I have missed her every day since she died and how I have longed to find you, Olivia. I searched, I went to the orphanage, only to be told that you had run away, and that they had washed their hands of you," Elizabeth said, and suddenly, she rushed to Olivia's side, throwing her arms around her, the two of them now sobbing in their embrace.

"It is a truly beautiful story," Lillian said, as tears rolled down Olivia's cheeks.

"Mrs. Mason, I fear we shall not make the theatre tonight," Sir Stanley said, but the housekeeper only laughed.

"I think we have had a far happier ending here tonight, sir, than we would have done at the theatre," she replied.

"We must have a toast, to new beginnings," Sir Stanley said, and he hurried to call the footman to bring champagne and glasses.

"What happens now?" Olivia asked, and Elizabeth smiled.

"You must come to know the family that is yours, Olivia, for I am certain that my mother and father would wish to meet you," she said, and Olivia glanced at Sir Stanley and Lillian.

"My family is under this roof, Elizabeth. I have always made my own family, wherever I have found myself, for what else could I do, not knowing the truth about myself?" she asked, and Lady Tupple nodded.

"I understand, but you must know that you are more than you ever thought you were, Olivia. You are no orphan, or pickpocket, or even servant in this house, but a lady and entitled to all which that entails," she said, as the footman returned with the champagne.

"But before all of that, let us offer a toast to the future and to extraordinary revelations," Sir Stanley said, as the champagne cork was popped and the bubbles fizzed.

"To discovering the truth," Elizabeth said, raising her glass, "and to my sister, who would have been so proud to know the daughter now discovered, a daughter I am proud to call my niece."

***

There was no theatre that night, not upon the stage at least, though as Mrs. Mason had suggested, the revelation of Olivia's true identity proved far more exciting than even *Macbeth*. The household was in a state of much excitement and uproar, none of them able to sit down to dinner, and all of them talking over the revelations, as further information came to light.

Elizabeth told them more of the family seat in Kent and that Olivia's mother was buried in the churchyard there. Her grandparents rarely spoke of their daughter, and it seemed there had been much shame on their part at the discovery of her pregnancy. Olivia did not think much of them for abandoning her in such a way and wondered how easy any relationship with them might be. She had Sir Stanley and Lillian for parents, and no better parents could be imagined. Did she really need grandparents too?

"But you must meet them, Olivia, they will want to see you," Elizabeth said, as the family sat in the drawing room over port and stilton a little later that night.

Olivia sat close to Arthur, who had been nothing but a comfort to her that night, and she was grateful for his presence, longing soon to be alone with him so that they might talk these extraordinary events over.

"But why did they send me away? You were but a child yourself and could have done nothing, but they surely could have raised me as their own," Olivia said, shaking her head.

"I think they realise they were foolish to do so. They did nothing to prevent me from searching for you. My mother even came with me to Craddock's Correction House to make enquiries, but Mr. and Mrs. Dounce were of little help," Elizabeth said.

"Mr. and Mrs. Dombus Dounce are amongst the most unreasonable of people. I was only glad to have gotten away," Olivia replied, and Elizabeth laughed.

"Yes, the lady in question told us you had caused an uproar with a mouse and that she could not show her face in the church since," Elizabeth said.

"And I would do it again, the horrible woman," Olivia replied, a grin coming over her face.

"You do not have to meet your grandparents if you do not wish to, Olivia. Lillian and I will support you in whatever you choose. We are your family and always shall be," Sir Stanley said, smiling at Olivia, who fought back the tears at these kind words.

"And this has always been my home. How easily you could have cast me away all those years ago and sent me back to Mr. Gobler," Olivia said.

"Mrs. Dounce mentioned a friend of yours, a … Mary Madeline or …" Elizabeth began, and Olivia looked up at her.

"Mabel Marie, yes, she and I were the closest of friends, but sadly I know nothing of her now, for she was left behind when I came to live here and I have known nothing of her since," Olivia replied.

She had always wondered about Mabel Marie and of all people, it was she that Olivia would dearly love to see again. Was she even still in London? Were Mr. Gobler and the others still living in the warehouse's attic practising the art of the pickpocket? It all seemed so long ago, another life and another world.

"Perhaps we might make enquiries. Your grandfather, my father, is a magistrate of some note. We may be able to find her," Elizabeth said, and Olivia smiled.

"I would like that," she replied.

They talked long into the night and Olivia learned more about her family and the grand house in Kent where she had been born. It seemed extraordinary to think of herself not as an orphan or a street urchin, the recipient of charity, but as a lady, with all which that entailed. As she made her way to bed later that evening, she could not help but dwell upon it, almost unable to believe the good fortune which was hers.

"Olivia, are you all right?" Arthur's voice came from behind her, and she turned to him and smiled.

"I had hoped we might talk alone," she said, and he hurried up the stairs to her side.

"Come, we can sit in the nursery like we used to," he said, and the two of them made their way into what was now the schoolroom where earlier that day they had sat declining verbs and learning geography, life now having changed irrevocably.

"I cannot believe that I know who my mother is, for I had spent so long thinking that I would never know I was," Olivia said, and Arthur reached out and took her hand.

"I had always known there was something special about you. You were not just a street urchin or an orphan, there was so much more to you than that. Now it is proved true," he said, as Olivia laughed.

They were sitting with a single candle to light the darkness, for the hour was now late, and Olivia looked at Arthur, wondering now what the future might hold for them.

"Do you think I should meet them? My grandparents, I mean. They abandoned me and would have disowned my mother if she had lived," Olivia said, shaking her head.

"Can people not change? Can they not have regrets? Elizabeth speaks of their sorrow and of how they tried to find you at the orphanage. Do they not deserve a second chance? Do you not deserve the family you have always longed for?" he asked.

"But I have that family right here, you and your father and mother, Mrs. Mason, you are all my family and I love you with all my heart," she said, and he smiled at her and squeezed her hand.

"As do we love you too, Olivia," he replied, and to her great surprise, he leaned forward and kissed her on the cheek, before sitting back with an embarrassed look upon his face.

"Which is why I am unsure if I need another family, even now I know of them," she replied, her cheek tingling in the aftermath of his touch.

"We shall support you in whatever you choose, and you and I will always be closest of friends," he whispered.

They sat together in silence for some time, as Olivia pondered all that had happened to her. When at last they bid one another goodnight, she found she could not sleep, her mind so full of thoughts and possibilities. But there was one resolve she now determined to see through, and that was to meet her grandparents and discover more of the truth about herself.

Chapter 16
Surprises in Kent

It was two days later, and there had been much correspondence between London and Kent. Elizabeth had written immediately to her parents with the news of her remarkable discovery and a letter had arrived by return of post, rejoicing in the news and asking Elizabeth and Olivia to come at once to Kent so that Olivia's grandparents might meet the granddaughter they had given up for lost.

"I would like Arthur to come too," Olivia said, when Elizabeth had explained the situation.

"He is very welcome to do so. Why not all the family, too?" Lady Tupple replied, looking around the breakfast table.

Sir Stanley paused, a forkful of devilled kidneys in hand, and glanced at Lillian, who nodded and smiled.

"We would be delighted. I have always loved Kent. It is so green and picturesque," she said.

"Then we shall make the journey this very day. The road is good, and a carriage will have us there in time for luncheon. There is no time like the present," Elizabeth said, and she rose from the table excitedly, "I am so glad you have chosen to meet your grandparents, Olivia, they have longed for this day, I assure you."

Olivia was nervous at the prospect of making the journey to Kent, but with Arthur, Sir Stanley, and Lillian at her side, she knew that all would be well. Soon, they were clambering into a waiting carriage outside, excitement brimming at the prospect of a journey into the countryside.

"The fresh air will do us all some good. It is months since we last left London," Lillian said, as the carriage pulled off along the street with a jolt.

"Is it a very big house?" Olivia asked, and Elizabeth smiled.

"Longcross Grange is a beautiful estate, I have always been happy there, though I wanted to know more of the world, hence my desire to take the position here, and how grateful I am that I did so," she replied.

They were soon crossing the river and making their way through Lambeth and out onto the road south. Longcross Grange was five miles north of Sevenoaks and it took them most of the morning to travel there, pulling through country lanes and past farms with fields of hops and wheat blowing gently in the summer sunshine. Olivia sat next to Arthur and despite her nerves, there was a sense of happiness about her too, happy knowing that she would soon know more of the home she had never thought herself to have.

"There is Longcross Grange, through the trees," Sir Stanley said, pointing from the carriage window, and Olivia looked out eagerly for a glimpse of the place she had been born.

It was a magnificent house, built in the Georgian style, with colonnades and a portico above steps rising from the forecourt. Two wings were built out at either side and the parklands contained mature trees and a boating lake, an island in the middle holding a folly, whilst an ornate bridge crossed the brook which flowed through the grounds, a drive leading up from the gates where two large stone lions stood guard on either side.

"I have never seen such a house," Olivia gasped.

"It rather puts our own to shame, but then we are only humble gentry, not like you, Olivia," Sir Stanley said, and Olivia laughed.

"I am but an orphan and a street urchin," she replied, and now it was the others who laughed.

"That is what you thought yourself to be, Olivia, but the truth is rather more exciting," Sir Stanley said, as the carriage pulled up outside the house.

A shiver ran through Olivia at the sight now before her. Despite having no recollection of Longcross Grange, she could not help but feel something of a connection to the place, a distant memory, as though she had been there before, which of course she had.

"It is wonderful, Olivia," Arthur whispered, and Olivia slipped her hand into his for reassurance, as several footmen now appeared to assist them.

"And there are your grandparents," Elizabeth said, and Olivia turned to see an elderly couple, arm in arm, standing at the top of the steps.

Her grandfather was an imperious looking man with a shock of white hair and a stern looking face, whilst her grandmother was equally grand, dressed in an elegant black gown and with a tiara perched upon her head. Olivia and the others stood at the bottom of the steps, as though awaiting a summons, as Elizabeth stepped forward.

"Mother, Father, may I present to you, Olivia, and how glad we are to be here," she said.

There was silence for a moment, and Olivia wondered if she had done the right thing in coming. Should she curtsey or make an apology for herself? She looked up and to her great surprise, it was not a stern face she saw, but tears. Her grandfather was crying, and her grandmother held out her hands, sobbing, as she tried to speak.

"Oh, Olivia, how much you look like your dear mother, you are her very image," she exclaimed.

"The very image, how sorry we are, Olivia. You must know that we had given up all hope of this happy day," her grandfather said, as the two of them helped one another down the steps.

Olivia stood meekly before them, unsure of what to say. She had been angry at first, confused why her grandparents had abandoned her. But, as Arthur had reminded her, it was possible for people to change, to regret the past and long to put it right. Olivia knew that all too well, her life as a pickpocket, a reminder that she herself had not always behaved as she might have liked.

"How foolish we were all those years ago, and how thankful we are to have finally found you," Olivia's grandmother said, and she stepped forward to embrace Olivia, who began to cry.

"This must all be strange for you," her grandfather said, placing his hand gently on her shoulder.

"I ... I am ... I am so pleased to know you," Olivia said, and she clung to her grandmother, as though she were embracing the past she had never known.

"You should know what a fine young lady your granddaughter is," Sir Stanley said, and Olivia's grandparents smiled.

"We owe you a debt of gratitude, Sir Stanley, for all you have done to take care of her. If it were not for you then there would never have been a chance of finding her," Olivia's grandfather said, holding out his hand to Sir Stanley, who shook it warmly.

"Tell me about my mother," Olivia said, and her grandmother smiled.

"We can do more than tell you, come this way, you must all need refreshment after your journey," she said, and the two of them led Olivia and the others up the steps and under the portico, through the doors and into a magnificent entrance hall.

They tiled it in black and white, a sweeping staircase rising from its centre and the walls covered in pictures and portraits. But it was a painting immediately above them which Olivia's grandmother now pointed to. It was the largest of them all, hung in pride of place, and it showed a woman, a woman who looked almost exactly like Olivia herself.

"Your mother, Beatrice, and now you can see why I was so astonished at the sight of you," her grandfather said.

"On that day when we first met, it was as though my sister had entered the room," Elizabeth said, slipping her arm into Olivia's.

"She is beautiful," Olivia gasped, gazing up at the portrait which showed a smiling woman, not much older than herself, dressed in a blue gown and seated beneath a rose trellis, the blooms so life like, that it seemed they could be plucked from the picture.

"There is no doubting who you are," her grandmother said, as Olivia gazed up, mesmerised by the portrait.

"You have every bit her beauty," Arthur whispered, his hand still clasped in Olivia's.

"Never in my wildest dreams did I imagine a truth like this," Olivia said.

"And we can only say again how sorry we are for the mistake we made in sending you away, it shames me to think of it," her grandfather said, shaking his head sadly.

"We did not know what to do, your poor mother. It was all too much. We regretted it, of course, and later we tried to find you, but to no avail," her grandmother said.

"I forgive you," Olivia whispered, turning to her grandparents, who once again could not hold back the tears.

"Oh, Olivia, what a truly remarkable woman you have become. You have overcome so much, and we shall always be here for you now, there is much to make up for," her grandmother said, and she embraced Olivia, kissing her, as she continued to lament.

Together, the family enjoyed a delicious luncheon, served in the spectacular dining room of Longcross Grange, where Olivia learned more about her mother, who by all accounts was a remarkable woman too.

"She was certainly feisty and would always have her own way. That is why we were so distraught over what had happened. Joseph Bayly was not an evil man, by any means. But society is what it is, and the scandal of what had occurred would have been too much to bear. Perhaps things are different now, but we did only what we thought best," Olivia's grandfather said.

"And there is no hope of ever finding my father?" she replied, and her grandmother shook her head.

"The last we knew of him, he was in Norfolk, labouring on the Sandringham estate, but that was many years ago," she replied.

"Though there is someone you might help us find, your Lordship," Sir Stanley said, and Olivia's grandfather nodded.

"If I can be of any service, then I shall be," he said.

"I know that Elizabeth … Lady Tupple, has told you about Olivia's past, but there is a particular friend she has always longed to know of, a Mabel Marie, her friend at the orphanage and then in London, perhaps you know of Artemis Gobler and his companions, the gentleman with whom Olivia lived for many years," and Olivia's grandfather nodded.

"I would hardly call Artemis Gobler a gentleman. He was amongst the most wanted men in all of London," he said, and Olivia looked up in surprise.

"Was?" she asked, and her grandfather nodded.

"Now residing in Belmarsh prison, and set to remain there for many years," he replied.

"But what became of the others? They were only children," Olivia said, gasping as she turned to Arthur.

"They were sent to the workhouses, but it should be no difficulty to find Mabel Marie. I shall do all I can," Olivia's grandfather said, and Oliva breathed a sigh of relief.

"May we help her? I have felt such guilt at leaving her behind these years past. I would truly love to see her again," she said.

"Then it shall be done, Olivia. Now, perhaps you and Arthur might like to see over the house. I am sure that Elizabeth would escort you," her grandfather said, and the three of them rose from the table and took their leave.

***

"It has been the seat of our family for a dozen generations, gifted us by the Stuart kings," Elizabeth said, as the three of them walked through the vast house, with its fine furnishings and exquisite portraits.

"I have never been in such an enormous house," Olivia said, gazing around her in awe.

"But it is the gardens which are most impressive. Designed by Capability Brown and added to by my grandmother. At this time of year they are quite remarkable," Elizabeth replied.

She led them along a wide gallery which ended in doors leading out onto a terrace, the gardens seeming to stretch endlessly before them. Below, a fountain stood at the centre of formal beds planted with roses and lavender, the scent from which was rising in the shimmering sun and perfuming the air. Lilac trees edged the walkways and a long pond, ended in a statue of a Greek deity, holding up a trident, as though posed in victory.

"Remarkable," Olivia gasped, turning to Arthur, who smiled.

"I should love to explore them," he said, and Elizabeth smiled.

"You do not need me to chaperone you, I am sure. Take these steps here and make a circle of the grounds, the fountain is a delight upon a hot day," she said, and Arthur offered Olivia his arm, the two of them smiling at Elizabeth, as they made down to where the lawns began.

"Your grandparents seem the most delightful of people," Arthur said, as they walked arm in arm through the box lined walkways, where the lilac trees blossomed on either side, their petals scattering in the gentle breeze, like confetti strewn in celebration.

"They are not as I expected. I imagined them to be stern and unforgiving, but they are nothing like that at all. If anything, they want only to make amends for the mistakes of the past. I was wrong to think of them in such a way," Olivia said.

"People change, you yourself are proof of that," Arthur replied.

"I feel no different, I am still Olivia, for I have been many things in the years that have passed," she replied, and he smiled.

"You will always be my Olivia," he said.

They had come to the fountain now, which gushed merrily up to a great height above, before falling back into the pond where ornamental fish swam beneath the clear, blue waters, and lily pads sat proudly with their white flowers in bloom.

"I wonder if Lady Tupple will still wish to teach us? I was enjoying her lessons and I do so want you to go to Oxford," Olivia said, as he took her by the hand and smiled.

"But I am not sure if I do," he said, and Olivia looked up at him in surprise.

"It is your dream, Arthur. It is all you have ever wanted. Why this change of heart?" she asked, and he smiled.

"Because, as I told you, change comes to us all. You have changed, I have changed, our circumstances have changed," he said, and Olivia's heart skipped a beat.

"But what do you mean?" she asked, and he took hold of her hand and knelt before her, the birds singing in the trees above and the fountain splashing musically behind.

"There is nothing now which holds us back. You and I can marry, if you wish it, that is. How I have loved you ever since I first laid eyes upon you in those far-off days of childhood and how that love has only grown in the years which passed. It is my only wish to marry you, Olivia, and I would gladly give up everything to do so. I love you, Olivia, with all my heart and how I long for you to say those words to me too. Marry me, Olivia, and let us be happy together forever, whatever the future might hold," he said, gazing up at her with imploring eyes, as tears rose in her own and her hands trembled.

"Can this truly be? I had never thought it possible, but you are right. There are no barriers. I had kept me feelings hidden, kept them back for fear of hurt. We knew we could never marry, not before. But now, there is nothing to prevent us, though I suppose I must ask permission from those I consider my true parents, your mother and father," she said.

"They will gladly give it. I have already spoken with my father and he agrees we would be the happiest of couples together. All that remains is for you to say yes, my dearest, Olivia," he said, and she gasped, the tears now flowing freely down her cheeks.

"Then the answer is yes, a thousand times yes. I love you," she gasped, and he rose to his feet, taking her in his arms and kissing her, as each of them now knew the delight of the happiness each had longed for and which sad circumstances had prevented.

"You have made me the happiest of men, Olivia, happier than I could ever have imagined. I would forgo everything, if only to be at your side, for the two of us to share the love we have each felt these long years past. Oh, how I have thought of this day, dreamed of this day, but never truly believed it would come," he said, and he swept her up in his arms, kissing her again, they walked together back toward the house, the wisteria scattering its petals in celebration and the sweet scent of roses in the air.

Chapter 17
The Guest of Honour

The news of Olivia and Arthur's engagement was greeted with much delight amongst the family. Olivia's grandparents insisted upon toasting the joyous occasion and champagne was called for. Olivia had never felt happier, for now she not only knew the truth about her family, but that truth had opened the way for her and Arthur to wed, a happier outcome than she could ever have hoped for. When they returned to London that night, Olivia had gone straight to Mrs. Mason to inform her of the good news and there had been further tears of rejoicing, as the housekeeper congratulated her upon the joyful news.

Much would need to be organised, and they agreed that the wedding would take place in London in the autumn, followed by a celebration at Longcross Grange. Olivia's mind was in a whirl, but she knew she had made the right decision and that she and Arthur would be happy together forever. As the day of the wedding arrived, she grew ever more nervous. It was to be a society occasion and both Sir Stanley and her grandfather, who had insisted upon financing the entire celebration, would give her away,

"You look beautiful, Olivia, it brings a tear to my eye," Mrs. Mason said, as she helped Olivia into her dress.

"My grandfather insisted that I have only the very best," Olivia replied, looking herself up and down in the mirror, and twirling.

The dress was of ivory satin, inlaid with pearls and lace trim, matched by a veil and tiara. She wore satin slippers, and a necklace given her by her grandmother, one which had belonged to her mother. It made her feel as though in some small way she was there too, smiling, as she watched her daughter ready herself for the wedding which she herself never got to enjoy.

"And the best is what you shall have, Miss Olivia. Now, the ultimate piece," Mrs Mason said, handing a pair of earrings to Olivia, which had been given her by Lillian and were also made of pearl.

"They are exquisite, are they not?" Olivia said, as she placed them on her ears, and gave a last glance in the mirror.

"Come now, the carriage will be waiting, and Master Arthur will grow nervous," Mrs. Mason said, smiling at Olivia.

Arthur had been nervous all week and Olivia had done her best to allay his fears, reminding him it was she he was marrying and not the rest of London society. Downstairs, she found Sir Stanley and her grandfather waiting in the hallway, each dressed in tails and top hats. Lillian had gone on with Arthur to the church and the two men now stepped forward to escort her, smiling at the sight of her making her way down the stairs.

"It brings a tear to my eye," her grandfather said, as Olivia now stood before them, and she could see that the same was true of Sir Stanley.

"Truly, you have blossomed into the finest of young ladies," he said, offering her his arm.

"And I could not have done so without you," she replied, taking his arm and that of her grandfather.

"You too, Mrs. Mason, you shall ride with us," Sir Stanley said, and today, he would not take no for an answer.

Outside, an open topped carriage was awaiting them, for it was still early in the autumn and the day was pleasant. Olivia was helped into the carriage by Sir Stanley and her grandfather, the two of them taking their seats proudly opposite her, as the carriage now departed for the church, with many people stopping to watch the delightful spectacle, applauding and cheering Olivia on her way.

"God bless you, ma'am, and may you know the joys of a happy marriage," one woman called out, and Olivia waved and smiled, as children ran after the carriage and further shouts of congratulation were given.

The steeple of Saint Michael's soon came into view and Olivia could see a small crowd gathered outside waiting to welcome her, at the front of which stood Lillian and her grandmother, grinning.

"Arthur is waiting inside, he is terribly nervous," Lillian said, as she embraced Olivia, the bells of the church ringing out above.

"He is not the only one," Olivia said, looking around her at the crowds which had gathered.

Her hands were trembling, just as they had done on the day that Arthur had asked her to marry him. She knew together they would be happy and that finally they had found the chance to be so. However, that did little to take away the nerves, or the beating of her heart, or the sense of all eyes being upon her.

"First, there is something else," Sir Stanley said, and Olivia looked at him in surprise.

"What else can there be? Are we not to begin the wedding now?" she asked, looking around her with a confused expression.

"But you have no bridesmaid, Olivia," Lillian said, adopting a serious tone.

"I had no one to take on that happy role," Olivia replied, growing ever more confused by their words.

"A lady cannot marry without a bridesmaid," Sir Stanley said, looking at her solemnly, and Olivia looked around her in alarm.

"Mrs. Mason, you could be a bridesmaid," she said, but the housekeeper shook her head.

"More like a maid of honour, Miss Olivia. Besides, it has taken Sir Stanley long enough to convince me to be a guest, let alone to follow you down the aisle," she said, and Olivia felt the panic rising within her.

"I … I do not understand," she said, but Sir Stanley suddenly smiled.

"We have found a bridesmaid for you, Olivia," he said, and turning, he pointed to the door of the church.

Olivia let out a cry of delight at the sight, for there, standing in the doorway, resplendent in a beautiful dress, was Mabel Marie. There was no mistaking her, though of course she herself was now a young lady, and she looked every bit the part, as beautiful as Olivia.

"Mabel Marie," Olivia gasped, and her friend rushed forward to embrace her.

"I thought I would never see you again, Olivia," she cried, tears running down her cheeks, as the two of them embraced.

"I have thought of you every day since we parted," Olivia said, holding Mabel Marie close, the two of them locked in an embrace.

"It was your grandfather who found me," Mabel Marie replied, and she told of how she had been sent to the workhouse, only to have been discovered by Olivia's grandfather. He found her lodgings and gave her an income to live on, Sir Stanley having promised to take her in as a help for Mrs. Mason.

"This is surely the best of wedding presents," Olivia said, turning to the others.

"But if we do not hurry, I fear the groom will be in great distress," Lillian said, as the bells continued to ring out over head.

"Of course!" Olivia cried, and Mabel Marie took up the train of her dress, as Sir Stanley and her grandfather offered her their arms.

The organ now thundered, and they made their way into the church, which was filled with guests and where Arthur was waiting by the altar. He turned now to look at her, beaming, as she came to stand at his side.

"I thought you were not coming," he whispered, as the rector now stood before them, his prayer book open.

"I had quite a surprise as I arrived," Olivia replied, glancing at Mabel Marie, who grinned.

And so, Olivia and Arthur were married, and there was much joy and celebration afterwards. Olivia had never been happier than in that moment, surrounded by her friends and family, reunited with all those whom she held dear and rejoicing in the happiness which was now hers.

"It is 'journeys end in lovers' meeting' as they say in *Twelfth Night*," Mrs. Mason said, outside the church afterwards, smiling at them both.

Olivia looked at Arthur, the two of them sharing a kiss, a happy future awaiting them, as the church bells rang out above them.

"The journey is only just beginning, Mrs. Mason," Olivia replied, taking Arthur by the hand, knowing that there was still so much joy to come.

"And we shall share it together, for life is better when shared with those we love," Arthur replied, and once more he kissed her, a shower of confetti covering them and the applause of all those whom they loved ringing out around them.

*** The End ***

If you enjoyed this story, could I please ask you to leave a review on Amazon? Thank you so much.

Printed in Great Britain
by Amazon